# The Bad Times of Irma Baumlein

# The Bad Times of Irma Baumlein

**by Carol Ryrie Brink**

illustrations by Trina Schart Hyman

**Aladdin Books**
Macmillan Publishing Company   New York
Maxwell Macmillan Canada   Toronto
Maxwell Macmillan International
New York   Oxford   Singapore   Sydney

First Aladdin Books edition 1991

First Collier Books edition 1974

Text copyright © 1972 by Carol Ryrie Brink

Aladdin Books
Macmillan Publishing Company
866 Third Avenue
New York, NY 10022

Maxwell Macmillan Canada, Inc.
1200 Eglinton Avenue East
Suite 200
Don Mills, Ontario M3C 3N1

Macmillan Publishing
Company is part of the
Maxwell Communication
Group of Companies.

Printed in the United States of America

A hardcover edition of *The Bad Times of Irma Baumlein* is available from Macmillan
Publishing Company.

1  2  3  4  5  6  7  8  9  10

Library of Congress Cataloging-in-Publication Data
Brink, Carol Ryrie, 1895–
The bad times of Irma Baumlein / by Carol Ryrie Brink;
illustrations by Trina Schart Hyman.—1st Aladdin Books ed.
p.  cm.
Summary: Irma's lie about having the biggest doll in the world
leads her into deeper and deeper trouble.
ISBN 0-689-71513-7
[1. Dolls—Fiction.]   I. Hyman, Trina Schart, ill.   II. Title.
PZ7.B78Bad  1991

[Fic]—dc20

91-13976
CIP
AC

*For Sarah
who first introduced
me to hamsters.
With much love!*

# Contents

# · I ·
# Judy's House

Irma Baumlein told a lie. It was the first bad thing that Irma had ever done, and all of the terrible things that she did later grew out of the lie, like poisonous mushrooms out of a rotten log.

Irma was walking home from school one autumn day with a bunch of books under her arm. She read a great deal, and she liked to go to the school library and take out books to keep her occupied in the long evenings in the big old-fashioned house where she lived. She was walking alone because she did not know many of the children in the new school she attended. They knew each other already, and they were not much interested in Irma. As for Irma herself, she couldn't care less if they wouldn't speak to her or be friends. She was sure that she would not like them anyway and—

But just then Judy Miller ran and caught up with Irma.

"Hi," she said.

"Well, hi!" said Irma, surprised out of her gloomy
thoughts.

"Can I walk along?"

"You *may*," said Irma, looking over the tops of her
glasses.

"What's your name?" asked Judy.

"It's Irma Baumlein."

"My gracious!" said Judy. "Are you Baumlein's Department Store?"

"Well, it's my great-uncle's store," said Irma. "My
father's come to help manage it." She thought later, after
she had told her lie, that she might just as well have told

Judy that her father *owned* the store. That's how one lie makes another easier.

"What's *your* name?" Irma asked.

"My name is Judy Miller, and I have four brothers and two sisters—one's just a teeny baby—and I have a little dog that shakes hands and rolls over and jumps over a stick, and I have a lot of hamsters. What do *you* have?"

Irma thought hard and fast. What did she have? No brothers and sisters, no little dog, no hamsters. Her mother was spending a month at a health spa, probably having her face lifted; her father was very, very busy trying to make things go better at Great-uncle Arnold's store; Great-uncle Arnold was at home with the gout; Great-aunt Julia was very deaf; and the Live-in Couple, who acted as maid and butler, frightened Irma half to death. She took so long to answer that Judy said, "Don't you have *anything?*"

Then Irma said (and she was surprised to hear herself say it), "Yes, I have the Biggest Doll in the World. She's as tall as I am. She's big enough to wear my dresses."

"Really?"

"Certainly."

"Where do you keep her?"

"I keep her in the closet across from my bed."

"Gee! Could I see her some time?"

"My mother doesn't like for me to take her out," said Irma. "She's quite breakable."

"I'd be awfully careful."

"Well, maybe sometime, when I know you better, Judy."

"My! How exciting to have a doll as big as that," said Judy. "Can she walk?"

"Yes, if I hold her hand," Irma said.

"What color is her hair? Is it black like yours?"

Irma pulled at one of her black pigtails tied with red yarn.

"No," Irma said, "her hair is the color of ripe oranges, and her eyes are cerulean blue."

"Cerul— what kind of blue is that?"

"It's the blue of the sky," said Irma, pursing up her lips and thinking how many big words she knew.

"Listen, Irma," Judy said. "Why don't you stop at my house on your way home? You do live in that great big Baumlein house on top of the hill, don't you?"

"Yes," Irma said. "It's really my Great-uncle Arnold's house, but as soon as we are settled we'll probably get something much, much nicer."

"Gee!" said Judy. "How could anything be nicer than the great big Baumlein house?"

Irma thought of the small pleasant apartment where she and her mother and father had lived so happily in New York before her father came to Tinkersville to manage Uncle Arnold's store. But somehow she felt that she could not tell Judy about that. The New York apartment was something familiar and kind but lost now and gone forever.

4

"Oh, there are nicer places," Irma said vaguely.

"Like what?" asked Judy eagerly.

"Oh, perhaps a château," said Irma.

"A chat— what is that?"

"A sort of palace, I suppose," said Irma, "with chandeliers and drawing rooms and a little green gazebo out in the garden."

Judy looked at Irma admiringly—all those big words that Irma knew, and what a wonderful house they conjured up in Judy's mind!

"Well," Judy said, "you won't think much of *my* house, but I'd like you to stop by anyway. You can see my little dog, and our baby if she's awake from her nap."

Judy's house was right on the way from school up the hill to the big Baumlein house. Unless she went through the park, Irma passed it every day, but she had never particularly noticed it. It was a small gray house like any other house in the block, only perhaps a little more cluttered. There was a baby carriage on the front porch and a small doghouse near the front door, and there were tools and old wooden boxes and pieces of wire screening lying around.

Two boys were at work building something with the tools and boxes and wire screening.

"That's Matthew and Mark," said Judy. "They're building a runway for the hamsters. Do you like hamsters?"

"I don't know," Irma said. "I never saw one."

"Well, I'll show you," said Judy. "They're something like mice, only cuter and without tails. If you have two or three of them, you soon have others, and then you have to build an extra runway, so they'll be happy."

"I see," said Irma. She looked over the tops of her glasses at Matthew and Mark, but they were too busy to pay any attention to a couple of girls.

Irma knew a rhyme that said,

"Matthew, Mark, Luke and John,
You saddle a rat, and I'll jump on."

It was a way you remembered the first books of the New Testament. Now she asked Judy, "Where are Luke and John?"

"They're probably out back playing croquet," Judy said. "But how did you know their names?"

"I guessed," said Irma.

"Be real quiet now, and you can look at our baby."

The two girls tiptoed onto the porch, and peered under the hood of the old-fashioned baby carriage. In a nest of blankets Irma saw a small round head, trimmed with a soft yellow fuzz of hair, eyes closed, cheeks pink. A small pink hand clutched at the blanket.

"She's nice, isn't she?" Judy said.

"Yes," said Irma. "Very nice."

In the house a lady was taking a pan of cookies out of the oven.

6

"Mama, this is Irma Baumlein. Her great-uncle owns Baumlein's store, and do you know what? Irma has the Biggest Doll in the World. It's as big as she is and it can wear her dresses."

"My! My!" said Mrs. Miller. "How are you, Irma?"

"Pretty well, thank you," said Irma shyly, looking over her glasses.

"Well, you may each have a cookie, but no more than one. These are for the P.T.A. Is your mama going to the P.T.A. tonight, Irma?"

"I don't think so," Irma said. "I expect she'll be going to the theater or a ball or something."

"Oh, yes, of course," said Mrs. Miller.

"Mama, Irma's doll has hair the color of ripe oranges, and cerul—you tell her, Irma, eyes."

"Cerulean," Irma said in a small voice.

"It means sky blue," said Judy.

"My! My!" Mrs. Miller said.

In the backyard two boys were trying to play croquet with an old croquet set; the balls had lost most of the colored stripes from being banged around too much. A small girl named Patty kept running after the balls and trying to pick them up. Anybody should know that croquet balls must not be picked up in the middle of a game.

A little dog who knew better than to chase croquet balls was sitting by looking interested. But when he saw Judy, he left the game and came running. His tail wagged, and his tongue lolled out of his mouth as if he were laughing.

"This is my dog, Orbit," Judy said. "I call him that because when he goes around and around after his tail, Daddy says he's in orbit. Do you know what an orbit is?"

"Certainly," said Irma.

"Would you like to see him do his tricks?"

"Yes, I would."

It was perfectly true what Judy had said. Orbit could shake hands and roll over. Then Judy held up a stick and Orbit jumped over it in one direction and then back again the other way.

"Now he'll say his prayers," Judy said. She pulled up

an empty box and told Orbit to sit up beside it. "Now say your prayers," she commanded. Orbit put his nose down on the box and covered his eyes with his paws.

"Stay," said Judy. Orbit stayed very still for almost a minute until Judy said, "Amen!" Then up jumped Orbit, barking with delight, and began chasing his tail.

Irma didn't often allow herself to show how interested she could be, but now she forgot about looking slightly bored. She cried, "Oh, he's a dear! He's cute! He's darling!" The little dog stopped chasing his tail and came up to her to be patted on the head.

"Oh, I wish I had a little dog like this," Irma said.

"But you've got your doll," said Judy. "I wish I had a doll like yours. Only I don't know where I'd keep it— our house is so small."

Then they went and looked at the hamsters in their cages near the back fence, and the hamsters were darling too. Judy took one out and let Irma hold it, and it was soft and funny. It twitched its nose and ran up Irma's arm, and she had to hold it in both hands to keep it from getting away.

"Would you like to keep it, Irma?" Judy said. "We have more of them than we need."

"Oh, yes," Irma said. "How would I keep it? What would I feed it?"

"You'd have to have a cage of some kind."

"There's an old birdcage in the attic," Irma said. "I saw it when Mr. Dillingham put our bags away."

"I should think a birdcage would do, and hamsters

like seeds and crumbs and things birds and mice eat. You might give it a little bit of peanut butter sandwich to-night until you can buy some hamster seeds tomorrow at the store."

"Well, thank you very, very much," said Irma. "You've certainly been nice to me, Judy."

"That's all right," said Judy. "Someday I'll come up to your house and you can show me your doll."

# · 2 ·
# Irma's House

Irma had quite a time getting the hamster home. First
she put him in her pocket, but he kept sticking his head
out, threatening to run away—and she had all of her
library books to carry too. Finally Irma set her books
down and made a little strait jacket around the hamster
with her scarf, so that she could hold him firmly. Then
she picked up her books and ran the rest of the way up
the hill to Uncle Arnold's house. There were stone steps
the last part of the way up, and Irma was all out of
breath when she reached the front door.

It would have been nice if she could have opened it
herself and scurried privately up to her own room. But
the big front door was always kept locked, and Irma
didn't have a key. She had to ring the old-fashioned
doorbell, and Mr. Dillingham, the butler part of the
Live-in Couple, would come and let her in.

This had always seemed an unnecessary bore to Irma,
but today it was a downright nuisance. Here she was,

all out of breath, with a pile of heavy books and a struggling hamster in her scarf. To make matters worse, she had a strong feeling that she had better not let Mr. Dillingham see the hamster. He was almost certain to disapprove.

Thirty years ago the Dillinghams had come from England to take care of the Baumlein mansion, and now they were as much a part of it as the older Baumleins were. They were much more a part of it than Irma and her father, who had been here only six weeks.

The doorbell echoed throughout the big house, and Irma had to pull it four times before anybody came.

The old house had been built by Irma's great-grandfather in 1898, when Baumlein's Store was the only department store in town. In fact 1898 was carved in the heavy stone of the front gable. The portico, where Irma stood, was loaded down with curlicues and filigrees of carved wood. These were doubtless intended to make the house look gayer and lighter, but so far as Irma was concerned, they only heightened the gloom. When Irma stood in front of the big door, pulling the bell, she felt as if the whole weight of stone that was hanging over her was about to drop. She was sure that in another moment she and the hamster would be crushed by 1898 stones coming down on them with a great clatter.

Fortunately, before this happened, there was a sound of measured footsteps coming along the hall inside the house, and Mr. Dillingham opened the door.

"Good afternoon, Miss Irma," he said. "I trust that school went well?"

"Oh, fine," said Irma, "thank you very much!" And she rushed by him and up the stairs to her room. Irma's room had belonged to several generations of Baumlein daughters, and each had somehow left her mark on it. The old-fashioned dressing table with chintz skirts had belonged to Gretchen, the plate-glass mirror on the outside of the closet door had belonged to Emily, and the modernistic mobile hanging from the high ceiling had been left by Yvonne. As yet Irma had not left her mark.

"Perhaps it will be a hamster's cage," thought Irma.

She put her books on the bed, and, still holding the hamster tightly in her scarf, she panted up the final stairway to the attic.

The attic was a large and dusty room crowded with shrouded furniture and old trunks and unguessed treasures, and there, on a cobwebby chest of drawers, sat an empty birdcage. Irma ran with it back to her room.

She had a little bathroom of her own opening off her bedroom, and now, taking the precaution of putting the plug in the drain, she released the hamster in the bath tub. Free of his strait jacket, he raced around gaily for a while. The sides of the tub were too slippery and steep for him to get out. Irma felt safe in turning her attention to the birdcage. It was rusty and dirty, but Irma soon had it clean and shining. She put several thicknesses of newspaper in the bottom of the cage and then she fastened the top part of the cage back onto the bottom part and tried the little door that opened on the side. It opened more easily than Irma liked, but still she felt sure that the hamster would not be able to open it for himself. She put water in one of the little cups and she promised herself to get seeds and peanuts for the other cup tomorrow.

Then she caught the hamster and put him into the cage through the little door. He raced around and around. "He's in orbit," Irma said happily. "Maybe I should call him Orbit Two." She had not felt so happy since she came to Tinkersville.

She was even bold enough to go down and beard Mrs. Dillingham in her den. Mr. and Mrs. Dillingham were having a spot of tea in the butler's pantry before they began to prepare dinner.

"Please, may I have a peanut butter sandwich?" asked Irma, looking shyly over her glasses.

"You'll spoil your dinner," said Mrs. Dillingham disapprovingly.

"I promise to clean my plate," said Irma.

"She promises to clean her plate," said Mr. Dillingham.

"Very well," said Mrs. Dillingham, "but I don't know what we are coming to nowadays when children are allowed to eat at all hours."

"I could make the sandwich myself," suggested Irma.

"Indeed not," said Mrs. Dillingham. "I am sure I

haven't kept this kitchen spotless for thirty years only to let children make their messes in it now. I'll make you a peanut butter sandwich myself, and I hope that you won't get crumbs around upstairs."

"Oh, no!" said Irma.

As soon as she had the peanut butter sandwich, Irma rushed upstairs with it. Orbit Two had been shredding up some of the newspaper in the bottom of the cage and making a nest of it. Irma opened the little door and put the whole peanut butter sandwich into the cage. At first the hamster seemed alarmed, then interested. Then he came out of his nest and broke off a dainty portion of the sandwich. To Irma's delight he sat up on his hind legs, holding it in his paws to nibble at it. His tummy

was white and his paws were just like tiny pink hands. His teeth were sharp and his jaws worked very fast. His cheeks kept getting fatter and fatter, and Irma realized that he was storing the food in them until he felt like swallowing it later on.

Irma was so interested in watching the hamster that she almost forgot to get washed and clean for dinner. When dinner was ready Mr. Dillingham struck a big gong that hung in the front hall.

It sounded like a sonic boom all over the house, and although Irma had been here for six weeks, she still jumped when she heard the gong. When Irma came down the stairs into the big front hall, her father was just helping Uncle Arnold to walk to the dining room.

"Hi, Irma," he said.

"Hi, Daddy!" Irma cried more gaily than she had done in weeks. Her father leaned down and kissed her on top of her head, and Irma would have thrown her arms around his neck but Great-uncle Arnold said, "Take care, Nephew, I nearly lost my balance then. You'll have to hold my arm and walk more steadily."

"Well, how did school go today?" asked her father.

"Oh, fine," Irma said. She wanted to go on and tell him all about the hamster, but there was Mr. Dillingham standing in the doorway and looking disapproving. There never seemed to be a moment when Irma and her father could be alone together.

Great-aunt Julia was already in the dining room, fussing with the flowers on the table.

"Well, Irma, I never heard you come in," she said. "I hope you didn't dawdle on the way home. And how did school go today?"

"Oh, fine," said Irma, thinking that people always asked her how school went today but never waited to hear the answer. Sometimes it seemed that they were not terribly interested in finding out. But now Great-aunt Julia said, "How was that? Speak out, dear, for goodness sake, speak out!"

"School went just fine, Aunt Julia," Irma cried in her loudest voice.

"Well, that's a little better, my child," said Aunt Julia. "I must say that one of the chief faults of people nowadays is that they mumble their words." Aunt Julia never admitted that her hearing might be poor, but she deplored the fact that all the other people in the world were losing their voices.

Irma's father smiled at her over the soup, and again over the rare roast beef; but they hardly had a chance to exchange a word because Uncle Arnold wished to hear everything that had taken place at the store that day, and Irma's father was the only one who could tell him. There was much talk of inventories and percentages and profits and losses. Irma knew how to close her ears to this kind of talk as if she had been as deaf as Aunt Julia.

She was thinking of the hamster and how cute he was when he sat up and held a bit of peanut butter sandwich in his tiny hands. But suddenly a change in the conversation made her tune in again.

"I noticed that you had a letter from Zena today, Nephew," said Aunt Julia in her odd, flat voice. "Did she say when she would be coming to join us?"

Irma was listening now with both of her ears, for Zena Baumlein was her mother. Her father cleared his throat and spoke quite slowly and loudly to Aunt Julia. "Zena sent her love to all of you," he said carefully, "but she won't be able to join us yet. The mural isn't quite finished, you see, and after that she will need a little rest."

"She could rest here quite as well as in New York," said Aunt Julia.

Irma looked anxiously at her father. She could see

18

that he was carefully choosing his words, and she knew why.

"There's a particular health spa in upper New York State that always relaxes her after she's had a busy season," he said.

"Humph!" replied Aunt Julia. "What kind of a woman did you marry anyway, Nephew?"

"The very finest!" said Irma's father loyally.

Irma was glad to hear him say it, but she knew that he was worried, and she was too. She couldn't help remembering the conversation she had heard before she and her father left New York.

Irma's mother, Zena Baumlein, was a mural artist, and although she was pretty and gay and kind and often jolly, she did not always see things the way other children's mothers did. Irma could still hear her mother saying to her father, "If you think that I am going to bury myself in your Uncle Arnold's gingerbread mausoleum, you are quite, quite mistaken."

(Irma knew gingerbread, but she had to look up mausoleum in her dictionary. It said: mausoleum, a burial place, an ornamental building erected to house the dead.)

"But, Zena," her father had said, "it probably won't be for long, and poor old Uncle Arnold needs me. The store is all out of date and somebody has to put new life into it."

"So why does it have to be you?"

"Because Uncle Arnold asked me, and because my father would have gone to help if he had been alive today."

"Very well," Irma's mother had said. "They'll take good care of Irma while you're busy at the store. And, as for me, I'll stay and finish the Humbolt mural, and, after that, I shall take a month or two at the health spa, and perhaps I'll even have my face lifted."

That was something that Irma could not find in the dictionary. The dictionary lifted loads of all kinds, but never faces. How did one look with a lifted face? Irma could not imagine. Sometimes she woke at night in a cold sweat and wondered if she would recognize her mother again if ever she should meet her. It was all very unsettling.

At the end of the steamed pudding with custard sauce, Irma looked over her glasses, and said, "I'd like to be excused and go to my room, please."

"Do you have something to read?" asked her father.

"Oh, yes, a pile of books."

"Shall I send up Mrs. Dillingham to open your bed?" asked Aunt Julia.

"*Oh no!*" cried Irma with more than usual loudness. "Thank you just the same, Aunt Julia."

Her father kissed her. "Be good, Daughter," he said fondly.

Irma knew that he would probably go back to the store, or that he would be busy in his own room with old ledgers full of figures. Uncle Arnold's store needed so much attention to bring it up to date!

The hamster was asleep in his nest when Irma turned on the light, but he poked his nose out and looked at her with his beady eyes. She took him out of the cage and let him run around her bed, and had a good time playing with him.

It was only after she had put him back in his cage and undressed herself for bed that another thought occurred to her. The dim lamp by her bed was the only light, and, as she walked toward the closet door to put away her clothes, Irma caught sight of herself in her long white nightgown in the mirror on the closet door. For a terrible instant she saw it—the life-size doll standing in the closet, the Biggest Doll in the World.

In the instant before she recognized herself, reflected in the mirror, Irma had a strong feeling of remorse. Her father had said, "Be good," and what had she done but tell an awful lie? She opened the closet door and there on the floor in a far corner sat a very small doll with her face to the wall. It was the only doll Irma had, and that was because she really did not like dolls very much anyway.

And now Judy Miller, who had been so kind to her, would want to see her life-size doll. What was she going to do? Irma could think of only one comforting possibility—perhaps Judy would forget.

# · 3 ·

# A Restless Night

In the middle of the night Irma woke up and began to worry. It was her usual time for worrying about her mother's face, but tonight she had two new things to worry her. First there was the lie she had told. What if Judy should insist on seeing the Biggest Doll in the World? How could she ever tell Judy the truth?

The second new worry that Irma had was the hamster. Since it was much pleasanter to think about the hamster than about the lie, Irma worried about the hamster. Was the birdcage too drafty for him? Did he have enough peanut butter sandwich? Would he be lonely for the other hamsters?

Since it was impossible to sleep with all of these anxieties going around in her head, Irma snapped on the light by her bed. She put on her glasses and her robe and slippers. Then she padded across the floor to the hamster's cage.

Unfortunately, what should have worried Irma most

of all had never even occurred to her. The door of the birdcage stood wide open. The hamster was gone!

In a panic Irma turned on all her lights and began to hunt in every nook and corner of the room. She looked under the chairs and under the chintz skirts of Gretchen's dressing table. She crawled under the bed, and she shook out the window draperies. She looked in all of her shoes that were neatly lined up against the closet wall. No hamster anywhere!

Finally Irma sat down on the side of her bed and gazed around her. Where could a hamster hide himself? Surely he couldn't get out of the room. Her eyes reached the door and traveled from the doorknob down to the floor, and she noticed, for the first time, that there was quite a sizable crack under the door. The old house had sagged here and there over the years. There were cracks under almost all of the doors.

Irma went down on her knees and stuck her finger in the crack, and she saw that an adventurous hamster would certainly be able to squeeze himself through it. Once out in that huge old house, he might be lost for days—perhaps forever.

While Irma was still on her knees, choking back her tears and wondering what she had better do next, there came a long, shrill cry from the end of the hall near the back stairway. It was followed by several short, shrill cries, and then a brief period of deadly silence.

Irma stood up and opened her door. She went cautiously down the hall toward the back stairway. There was a wide crack of light under the last bedroom door on the left, and when the cries began again, Irma was sure that they came from there.

Irma knocked on the door but no one came to open it.

"Help! Help! Take it away!" cried the shrieking voice. With a shock of surprise, Irma recognized the voice as that of Mrs. Dillingham. The idea of Mrs. Dillingham screaming for help rather pleased Irma's fancy. She knocked again, and when there was no answer, she cautiously opened the door and looked in.

Mrs. Dillingham was standing, or perhaps it would be better to say that she was dancing, in the middle of her bed. She had her nightgown clutched around her bony knees, and her head was bristling and spiky with large pink hair curlers.

"Help! Help! Take it away!" she screamed.

Mr. Dillingham, in an old-fashioned nightshirt, was racing madly around the room waving a broom. Irma saw at once that he was chasing her hamster, and she began to run after Mr. Dillingham, shouting: "Stop! Stop! You're going to hurt him. Oh, don't hit him with the broom! Don't!"

All together they made quite a hubbub.

Just then Irma's father and Uncle Arnold arrived and crowded into the open doorway. Deaf as she was, even Aunt Julia heard the screams and came to see what she could do to help.

"Dillingham, I am surprised at you," boomed Uncle Arnold. "Never strike a woman with a broom, man, especially your wife. It's very bad form, very bad form indeed."

"Ye-e-e-s, s-sir," stammered Mr. Dillingham, but he did not stop chasing the hamster.

"This is dreadful," said Aunt Julia, "taking your exercises in the middle of the night, Dillingham. You ought to be sleeping."

"We were!" cried Mrs. Dillingham, "until something ran over my face. It was all soft and furry—oh! oh! oh! and its feet were cold."

Mr. Dillingham, panting very hard, came to a stop before Uncle Arnold. "I'm extremely sorry, sir," he said, "but Mrs. Dillingham has an aversion to mice."

"Well, whatever she has an aversion to, you should not beat her for it, my good man."

"*Lice*, did you say?" cried Aunt Julia incredulously. "We've never had lice in this house."

"It's not a mouse at all!" Irma cried.

"A rat then," said Mr. Dillingham. "It must be a rat."

"No! No!" said Irma. "It's not a rat."

"Irma," said her father sternly, "what do you know about this?"

"Daddy," Irma said, looking at her father over the tops of her glasses, "I couldn't help it. It's my hamster. He got out of his cage."

"Her *what?*" asked Aunt Julia.

"Hamster," shouted Irma.

"Just as I thought," Aunt Julia said, "it *must* be a monster to make a sensible person like Mrs. Dillingham go into such a fit."

"Irma," her father said, "how does it happen that you have a hamster?"

"Judy Miller gave him to me," Irma said, "and he wouldn't hurt *anyone*—not even Mrs. Dillingham."

"He ran over my face," said Mrs. Dillingham with a shudder. But she had stopped screaming, and she was beginning to remember that she was a very dignified and proper person who made a business of frightening little girls the age of Irma.

While they were talking the hamster had stopped running, and now he sat up on his hind legs in a corner of the room. Irma could see that he had a crumb of something in his tiny pink hands. He clutched it against his furry white stomach. Then he began to nibble it daintily, all the time watching them with his beady eyes to see that they didn't start chasing him again.

"Oh, dear," wailed Mrs. Dillingham, "he's stolen my biscuit. I always bring up a glass of milk and a biscuit in case I get hungry during the night."

"I don't know what we are coming to when people are allowed to eat at all hours!" boomed Uncle Arnold.

Irma wanted to laugh, but instead she said, "No wonder he came into this room. He must have smelled the biscuit."

"You shouldn't have food in your bedroom, Mrs. Dillingham," said Aunt Julia in her flat voice. "It's bound to attract monsters."

"Irma," said her father, "please see if you can catch this hamster."

"Yes, Daddy."

The hamster scurried around a bit before he let Irma take him. But after all, he knew Irma pretty well now and trusted her. Finally he let her catch him and put him in her pocket.

"I thought you said it was a monster," complained Aunt Julia. "It's only a mouse!"

"No! No!" cried Irma. "It isn't a mouse. It's a hamster. It doesn't have a *tail*."

"Yes, I'm sure the biscuit must be *stale*," said Aunt Julia, "but there's no use screaming about it. Let's all go to bed now. And, Dillingham, be sure that my orange juice is well chilled for breakfast."

"Yes, madame. Yes, indeed, madame," said Mr. Dill-

ingham with the kind of bow he made when, in his
white gloves and tails, he passed the canapés.

"Where did this mouse come from?" asked Uncle
Arnold, looking at Irma's father.

"I believe my daughter owns it," Irma's father said.

"My friend, Judy Miller, gave it to me," Irma said,
"and it's a hamster, Uncle Arnold."

"Well, mouse or hamster, whatever it is, take it back
tomorrow, child. We can't have it running loose, scaring
the servants into fits."

"But, Uncle Arnold, I'll keep it in a cage," begged
Irma. "Please."

"Take it back," said Uncle Arnold. "You heard me say it. Take it back tomorrow. Now, Nephew, help me to bed, please. What a fuss over nothing."

"Daddy," begged Irma, "must I take it back?"

"I'm sorry, Irma, but you heard what Uncle Arnold said."

"And furthermore," said Uncle Arnold, addressing Mr. Dillingham, "I never want to hear that you have beaten your wife again, Dillingham. It's a very cruel thing to do, especially with a broom."

There was really no use in trying to explain to Uncle Arnold that Mr. Dillingham had not been beating his wife. Uncle Arnold had heard her screams and seen Mr. Dillingham running around waving a broom. So that was final.

With a deep sigh, Irma realized that it would be just as impossible to convince Uncle Arnold that she would keep the hamster locked in its cage from now on.

She went sadly back to her room and put the hamster into the cage. She took one of the red yarn strings that she wore on her pigtails and securely tied the door of the birdcage shut. She tied it so securely that no hamster in the world could push or gnaw it open.

"Good night, Orbit Two," whispered Irma. "Good night, good night, dear hamster. I'll have to take you back to Judy's in the morning."

Before she turned out the light, Irma had to polish her glasses because they were all fogged up with tears.

# · 4 ·
# How Was School Today, Irma?

The next morning at breakfast Irma found that she was not nearly so much in awe of the Live-in Couple as she had been. When you know that a person like Mrs. Dillingham is afraid of mice and has to take milk and a biscuit to bed with her, or that another person like Mr. Dillingham can chase a poor little hamster all around a room with a broom and never catch it, you begin to feel sorry for them, and they seem far less terrifying.

Nevertheless Irma was not cheerful as she prepared for school. She got her books all together—she hadn't looked at one of them. Then she took Orbit Two out of the birdcage and put him in the bathtub with the stopper securely closed. She tidied up the bits of torn paper and dried sandwich and put them in the wastebasket. After returning the birdcage neatly to the attic, she put on her coat and cap and polished her glasses (they would keep misting up!). Last of all she made a little strait jacket out of her scarf and secured the hamster in it. Then she ran down the hill as fast as she could go to the Millers' house.

When she rang the doorbell Mrs. Miller came to the door. Irma could hear the baby crying and the telephone ringing and the dog barking, and Mrs. Miller looked as if she was in a big hurry.

"Well, hi," she said. "You're the child who has the life-size doll, aren't you?"

"Ye-es, ma'am," said Irma faintly.

"Judy and the boys have left for school, dear. If you run fast you may catch them."

"It's not that," Irma said unhappily. "I've come to return the hamster."

"The what? Oh, but we have more hamsters than we need, dear. I'm sure that Judy meant for you to keep it."

"But I can't," said Irma desperately. "I would like to very much, but they won't let me."

"Dear! Dear!" said Mrs. Miller. The telephone continued to ring, the baby to cry and the little dog to bark. Irma could see that Patty, the next to the youngest, was putting croquet balls into the flour bin. "Well, I suppose if you can't keep him, you can't keep him," said Mrs. Miller finally. "I'm rather busy at the moment, dear. Would you just take the hamster out to the back yard and put him in the cage with the others?"

"Yes, ma'am," Irma said.

She ran around the house and unlatched the hamster cage. She removed the strait jacket and thrust Orbit Two in among the other hamsters. For a moment Irma stood looking at them, and she thought that Orbit Two was the handsomest one of them all. His vest was whiter, his brown back silkier, and his tiny hands pinker than any of the others. He sat up and looked at her in surprise, as if he did not expect to find himself back with his relatives so soon. Irma could not bear to stay longer. She picked up her books and dashed away down the hill, hardly looking where she went because her glasses were so foggy.

Before she reached the schoolyard, however, she slowed down and polished her glasses and walked along quietly so that no one would notice her. No one ever did notice her anyway, of course, so it was hardly worth the bother of trying to look bored, but she did it from force of habit.

But the air had changed this morning. It was full of a brisk hint of frost. Warm October was over and November was crisping the air. Everything else seemed to be topsy-turvy too. As soon as Irma's foot touched the school ground someone was calling her name.

"Irma! Irma Baumlein!" Irma could not believe her ears. What a wonderful sound to hear people calling her name! And then a whole flock of girls of about her age came rushing all around her.

"Here she is!" Judy said. "What did I tell you? It's the girl who owns the Biggest Doll in the World. It's Irma Baumlein."

"Do you really?" they asked. "Can she really wear

your dresses? Is her hair the color of ripe oranges? And what color are her eyes? Judy couldn't remember."

"Her eyes are cerulean blue," murmured Irma in a very small voice. "Yes, I do. Yes, she does. Yes. Yes."

Irma felt as if she were sinking gradually into the hard-packed ground of the schoolyard. But she only sank so far and the girls were all around her holding her up by her arms, carrying her books for her, propping her up from the back and making sure that she didn't disappear. Irma was dizzy with happiness at being loved by so many new friends, but she was also full of anguish at the thought that if she told them the truth they would all go away again and never notice her any more. "Yes," Irma said. "Yes. Yes. Yes."

A few boys stood around the edge of the group of girls and made fun of them. Irma saw Judy's brother Luke scoffing at them.

"I don't believe it at all," he said. "She's making it all up."

"Oh, no, she isn't!" cried the girls. "You aren't making it up, are you, Irma?" Dumbly Irma shook her head.

"You do have the Biggest Doll in the World, don't you, Irma?"

Irma nodded, but her eyes behind her shiny glasses followed Luke as he walked disdainfully away. She was not sure that she liked him, but she could not help feeling glad that there was one person in the world who did not believe her.

Things quieted down as soon as school started. Miss Oglethorp was a very nice teacher and Irma really enjoyed school. It was even pleasanter than usual today because the girls kept smiling at her, and they all came around her again at recess and took her into their games. Irma began to feel that, after all, Tinkersville might be a good place in which to live. Now she had all these new friends and very soon they would forget that she was supposed to own the Biggest Doll in the World. It would all be lovely.

The recitations went well and at the end of the afternoon there was a little extra time left before the bell rang.

"How would you like to discuss plans for your part in the Harvest Home Carnival?" asked Miss Oglethorp.

"Yes! Yes! Yes!" the children cried.

Irma did not know what the Harvest Home Carnival was, but she soon learned that it was an exciting thing which took place on an evening in November every year at the Washington School. Each room put on a display of hobbies, or an exhibit of handicrafts, or a play or an entertainment of some sort. Parents and friends paid to get in, and the money that was collected was used to buy new books for the library.

"Maybe we could give an art show," said Peter Simpson, who was always drawing pictures.

"Oh, no," said Henry Jones, "let's show our model airplanes."

"Most of us don't draw or make model airplanes," said Judy. "How about giving a play?"

"Who wants to act in a play? How about a food booth where we could sell ice cream and cake?"

"Where would we get the money to buy ice cream and cake?"

"The girls could make the cakes."

"Let's have a cat show," "A pie-eating contest," "Bicycle races," "A magician with card tricks!" Everybody talked at once except Irma, who had never been to a Harvest Home Carnival and didn't know what was expected of her.

Finally Miss Oglethorp clapped her hands. "One at a time, please," she said. "You'll never decide anything if you all talk at once."

Mary Hogan put up her hand.

"Yes, Mary?" said Miss Oglethorp.

"Maybe we could have a booth where we showed our greatest treasures. Peter could bring the best picture he has drawn, and Henry could bring his best model airplane, and Rodney could do his card magic, and Judy could bring her little dog and have him do his tricks, and I could bring my Siamese cat."

"Hey, the dog would chase the cat," cried Henry gleefully. "Wouldn't that be fun?"

"No," said Mary, "I'd have my cat in the cage she stays in at cat shows."

"Besides Orbit wouldn't chase a cat if I told him not to," Judy said.

Suddenly Irma heard herself saying in the kind of loud voice she used for Great-aunt Julia, "Maybe we could have a cage of hamsters!"

Everybody turned around and looked at her, and Judy cried out in surprised delight, "Irma! Irma Baumlein! I almost forgot about Irma Baumlein. Irma can bring the Biggest Doll in the World!"

There was a moment's silence and then everybody cried, "Yes! Yes!" Even the boys were interested. Dolls might be dull, but the Biggest One in the World! That would be something else.

"What's this about the Biggest Doll in the World?" asked Miss Oglethorp.

"Oh, Miss Oglethorp," Judy cried, "Irma has her. She's as big as Irma is and she can wear Irma's clothes. She walks if you hold her hand, and her hair is the color

36

of ripe oranges. And her eyes, her eyes are cerulious blue!"

"Cerulious?" asked Miss Oglethorp. "What color is that, Judy? Or maybe I should ask Irma?"

"She means cerulean," said Irma in a small voice.

"That's a very good word, Irma," said Miss Oglethorp. "Does anyone else know what it means?"

"It means sky blue," said Judy. "And just think, we could have the doll behind a screen with a big sign that Peter would make, saying, THE BIGGEST DOLL IN THE WORLD, ten cents. Everyone would want to see her, and think of all the extra ten centses we could make for the library fund."

"Ten cents is too much to charge to look at a doll," objected Henry.

"Well, five cents then. Surely anybody would pay five cents to see the Biggest Doll in the World."

"What does Irma say about this?" asked Miss Oglethorp.

They were all looking at Irma. This was the time to tell them! If there had only been one or two of them, but there were so many, and their eyes were boring holes in her. These were all her new friends who had come to meet her and had taken her into their games. Irma swallowed three times, and no words would come out of her dry mouth. Finally she swallowed again, and said in a very small voice, "I doubt whether my mother would let me bring her. She is very breakable."

Everybody groaned, and the girls all cried, "Ask her!

Ask her! Tell your mother we'll be very careful, and tell her how much we will make for the library fund."

"Tell her," said Mary, "that they give out blue ribbons and that the class that makes the most money for the library fund each year gets to keep the picture of *Washington Crossing the Delaware* all next year in their room."

"Irma is new," Miss Oglethorp said kindly. "Perhaps she doesn't know about the picture. Will you tell her, Peter?"

"Well," said Peter, "you see, our school, the Washington School, was the very first school in Tinkersville. I don't mean this building, because this is new. That's because the first building burned down, and the only thing that was saved was the picture of *Washington Crossing the Delaware*. So now everybody wants the honor of having that picture in his room."

"Or *her* room," said Judy, "and the only way to settle it is to let one room have it for a year and then another room will get it."

"And the way we decide which room gets it," said Henry, "is we see whose booth at the Harvest Carnival makes the most money for the library fund."

"I see," said Irma, polishing her glasses.

"So, if you tell your mother all this, I'm sure she'll let you show your doll," Mary said.

"I will ask her," Irma said.

That afternoon Irma forgot to go to the library to get her books. Her new friends all wanted to walk Irma home, but Irma felt that she must be alone to think things out.

"I have an errand to do," she said. That was not a lie, because she needed to go around to the grocery store and buy a package of bubble gum. If she had had a hamster, she would have gone to the pet store to buy a package of bird seed. She went home by way of the park. The trees were almost leafless now, but there were still clumps of green bushes, and a few very late chrysanthemums still bloomed in the flower beds. The park had been given to the city by Irma's great-grandfather, Jacob Baumlein, and it sloped up the hill from the Baumlein store to the top where the old Baumlein house stood.

Across from Baumlein's Store, where the park began, there was a bronze bust of Jacob Baumlein mounted on a stone pedestal. Carved in the stone were the words JACOB BAUMLEIN, A MAN OF INTEGRITY.

Irma did not need to go to the dictionary to find out about *integrity*. She knew that it meant that Jacob Baumlein had been honest. He looked stern too, and as if he would not much care for untruthful granddaughters.

Halfway up the hill, Irma sat on a park bench to rest. She took out a purple ball of bubble gum and began to chew it, but it did not cheer her.

"What am I going to do?" Irma said to herself. "What am I going to do?"

# 5

# BEEP

As usual, that night at dinner Irma's father and great-uncle Arnold talked about the business of the store.

"The shipments of Christmas toys are beginning to come in," said Irma's father. "We should have a very nice assortment this year."

"Well," said Uncle Arnold, "I hope that you have ordered a lot of toy trains and dolls. Boys always want toy trains and girls want dolls."

Irma's father cleared his throat. "Actually, Uncle," he said "we must realize that times are changing since you were young. Now it seems that boys want airplanes and space ships and model cars, and little girls want doctor's or nurse's kits and monster-makers and stuffed tigers."

"What about the dolls?" asked Irma breathlessly.

"You see," said Uncle Arnold triumphantly, "*she* still wants dolls. I expect the boys still want trains too. We mustn't get too modern in the store, Nephew."

"Why, yes, Irma," said her father, "we do have a shipment of dolls coming in."

"Very large ones?" asked Irma.

"Dolls that walk, dolls that talk, dolls that drink water out of a bottle and have to have their didies changed—"

"But are they *large?*"

"Oh, I'm sure that there must be large ones," said her father.

"If you are talking about dolls," said Aunt Julia, "and I guess you are, although nobody speaks up clearly these days—when I was a child I had a very large doll, it must have been the largest doll in the world."

Irma nearly jumped out of her chair. "Oh, Aunt Julia," she cried in a loud voice, "the largest doll in the world?"

"Well, I'm sure it was very large," Aunt Julia said. "Her name was Bertha Evangeline Esther Peebles— Peebles was my name before I married Baumlein. I daresay she's still in the attic, if you'd care to see her."

"Oh, I would care to very, very much!" cried Irma.

"I never knew that you were so interested in dolls, Irma," said her father. "You always asked for books or chemistry sets or stuffed animals. I didn't know—"

"This year," said Irma, looking over her glasses, "I am becoming very interested in large dolls."

"Then you must come down and look over our stock as soon as it is unpacked," said her father. "You are always welcome at the store, Daughter."

"I expect," said Irma in a small voice, "that a very large doll would be quite expensive."

"We haven't marked the prices on them yet," her father said, "but the larger they are, the more they are likely to cost."

After dinner Irma went along the hall with Aunt Julia. "Aunt Julia," she said in a loud voice, "do you think that I could see your large doll?"

"You mean Bertha Evangeline Esther Peebles?" asked Aunt Julia.

"Yes. Yes," said Irma. "Do you think that she is really in the attic?"

"Well, I certainly hope so," said Aunt Julia. "If Dillingham has thrown her out, I shall be extremely annoyed. As a little girl I was quite devoted to my dolls."

"Could we look for her tonight, Aunt Julia?"

"You mean Bertha Evangeline Esther Peebles?"

"Oh, yes, Aunt Julia."

"Well, I don't see why not. Run to the kitchen, Irma, and tell Dillingham that I shall require his services as soon as he has dried the dishes."

"Yes, Aunt Julia," said Irma breathlessly.

"Tell him," continued Aunt Julia, "to bring a flashlight, and a can of Flit in case the moths have been at her hair."

"What color is her hair?" asked Irma eagerly.

"Brown, of course," said Aunt Julia, "and very nice and curly, I'm sure the moths would love it."

"But, if the moths had been at her wig, Aunt Julia, perhaps we could get her another one, one that was the color of ripe oranges."

"What kind of nonsense is that, Irma? Brown is a very nice color."

"And her eyes?" asked Irma anxiously.

"I can't remember," said Aunt Julia. "Now run along and fetch Dillingham or it will be time for bed."

When Irma entered the kitchen Mr. Dillingham was in his shirt sleeves folding a damp dishtowel and hanging it behind the stove. Mrs. Dillingham was preparing her biscuit and her glass of milk on the best Haviland china tea plate.

"Well, well!" said Mr. Dillingham. "And how did school go today, Miss Irma?"

"Just fine," said Irma, because she knew there was no use trying to tell him anything else. "Mr. Dillingham, Aunt Julia wants you to take a flashlight and a can of Flit and go up to the attic with her to find Bertha Evangeline Esther Peebles."

"*Tonight?*" cried Mr. and Mrs. Dillingham in voices of consternation.

"We're in quite a hurry," Irma said. "It's really a sort of emergency."

"Very well, Miss Irma," said Dillingham, putting on his coat with the tails, "but it's very irregular I'm sure."

"Please hurry, Mr. Dillingham," Irma said.

Aunt Julia led the way up the attic stairs. "I know just which trunk she's in, Dillingham," Aunt Julia said.

"It won't be any trouble at all."

"I expect it will have to be a very large trunk, Aunt Julia," said Irma hopefully.

"Yes, yes, quite a small one, dear," Aunt Julia said. "There Dillingham, you will only have to move those three large trunks, and the mahogany dresser with the broken mirror. Bad luck to break mirrors, I always say, eh, Dillingham?"

While Mr. Dillingham was obediently moving trunks, Irma looked around her. The attic was poorly lit by one small light bulb hanging by a wire. But the gleam of the bulb picked out the shining wires of the birdcage and made Irma's heart thump. Oh, to have the smallest and furriest of hamsters clasped in her hand instead of the biggest of all the big dolls in the world! Oh, to have Orbit Two down in her cozy room once more and not a worry in the world! For a moment Irma was lost in dreams.

"There it is!" cried Aunt Julia. "That's Bertha Evangeline Esther's trunk, I'm sure. Open it, Dillingham."

"Yes, madame."

Irma came and stood beside Aunt Julia. The trunk was not large at all.

When Mr. Dillingham raised the lid, a strong smell of camphor balls floated out.

"Good!" said Aunt Julia. "We put her down in camphor balls, so we shan't need the Flit after all. Take her out, please, Dillingham."

Removing several layers of yellowed tissue paper, Mr. Dillingham lifted a large, old-fashioned doll out of the trunk. Large? Well, perhaps the size of a very large baby or a rather stunted two-year-old. Yes, certainly large, but she could never wear Irma's dresses. She could never qualify as the Biggest Doll in the World.

Irma felt her glasses beginning to fog over, but she knew that, no matter what, she should be sincerely grateful to Aunt Julia and Mr. Dillingham for all the trouble they had gone to.

"She's—she's very nice," Irma said. "Oh, thank you! Thank you! But she really isn't very large, is she?"

"Not large?" said Mr. Dillingham, under his breath. "For a doll that ugly, I'd say she was immense!"

"What's that?" asked Aunt Julia. "Speak up! Please don't mumble."

"Oh, Aunt Julia," Irma shouted. "Thank you! Thank you! Now that I've seen her, you can put her back."

"Put her back? Certainly not, dear child. She's been waiting all these years for another little girl to love her. Indeed not! Dillingham, there's a small chair for her to sit on behind the washstand. Get it out and take it down to Miss Irma's room, please. And Irma, dear, here she is—your own big dolly. Take her in your arms, dear, and love her."

Irma received the hard, unyielding body of Bertha Evangeline Esther Peebles into her arms and looked at her. She had brown curly hair, enormous brown eyes, fat cheeks, a small nose, and the tiniest cupid-bow

mouth that could be imagined. Peeping out from this tiny mouth were two small teeth like the tiniest pearls on a graduated necklace. Her joints made a creaking sound when Irma moved her arms or legs, and her eyes made a click whenever they opened or closed. And she smelled like camphor balls.

"Isn't she a darling?" cried Aunt Julia. "I had a cradle for her, as well as the little chair, and I had a small table and a tea set with pink roses on it. I used to try to feed her crackers, but her mouth was so tiny, she wouldn't take the smallest crumb. You may have her, dear. I give her to you. Play with her to your heart's content."

Irma saw that Aunt Julia had really loved her doll very much. Suddenly, for the first time, Irma loved Aunt Julia. She put up her arms and gave Aunt Julia a kiss.

"I will take good care of her," she shouted.

So, instead of a hamster cage, Irma now had a small-ish large doll sitting in her room in a little wicker rocking chair and the whole room reeked of camphor balls. There was nothing that Irma could do about this. But there was something that she could do about the name Bertha Evangeline Esther Peebles. "I'll call her BEEP," said Irma to herself.

She felt that she could never take BEEP to school, however. No one would believe that this was the doll with cerulean eyes and hair the color of ripe oranges— the Biggest Doll in the World. Irma's problem was as great as ever.

# · 6 ·
# The Window Trimmer

It was useless to go to Baumlein's Store until the holiday toys were unpacked, and Irma knew that this would take several days. In the meantime, however, the girls at school kept asking Irma when she would know if she could bring her doll to the Harvest Home Carnival.

"Have you asked your mother, Irma? What did she say? Will she let you or not?"

"She is thinking about it," Irma said.

"But we would like to know. Everyone else is making plans."

"I'm sorry," Irma said. "I can't hurry her."

"I know!" Judy said. "We'll get Miss Oglethorp to telephone her. I'm sure your mother would say yes to Miss Oglethorp."

"Oh, no," Irma said. "Don't ask Miss Oglethorp to call her. It—it might make her head ache."

"That would be too bad," said Mary, "but still we really want to know."

"Please wait a little longer," Irma said.

In her imagination Irma could hear Miss Oglethorp calling the Baumlein mansion. "Is Irma Baumlein's mother there? I should like to speak with her, please." And Mr. Dillingham would say, "Sorry, madame, there must be some mistake. Miss Irma's mother is in a health spa in upper New York State having her face lifted."

"Maybe I have the wrong number," Miss Oglethorp would say. "Is this the home of the Irma Baumlein who has the Biggest Doll in the World?"

"Sorry, madame," Mr. Dillingham would say. "There is only one Irma Baumlein, but you are quite mistaken about the size of the doll. Bertha Evangeline Esther Peebles is only about the size of a large baby. But, if you want to know, she's so ugly that she seems immense—"

"Oh, no!" Irma said to the. girls. "Don't ask Miss Oglethorp to call, *please*. I'll ask my mother again."

The time of the Harvest Home Carnival came closer and closer. The principal's office was getting out letters of invitation for the children to take home to the parents.

Peter Simpson had already made an elegant sign that said:

SEE THE BIGGEST DOLL IN THE WORLD

5¢

Mary had borrowed a screen to put around the doll.

"Please tell your mother to hurry and decide," Judy said.

The Carnival was to be on a Tuesday. On the Friday before, the letters of invitation to the parents were brought around to the various rooms and handed out to the children to take home.

One of the invitations was laid on Irma's desk. With a sinking heart she took it up and examined it. On orange-colored paper (the color of ripe oranges) was printed a drawing of pumpkins and sheaves of wheat. Beneath this it said:

### INVITATION to PARENTS

Please come to the Harvest Home Carnival
at the Washington School at 7 o'clock
on Tuesday, November 10th.

You will have
FUN, EXCITEMENT, ADVENTURE.

There will be games, tests of skill, food and entertainment. You will see displays of art, hobby collections, trained animals, and

THE BIGGEST DOLL IN THE WORLD.

Bring your quarters and your dimes for the benefit
of the School Library Fund.

Come one! Come all!

Why, oh, why had they printed that about the Biggest Doll? She hadn't even told them for sure that she could bring it. Irma's heart sank further and further until it seemed to be in the bottoms of her shoes.

Judy whispered across the aisle, "Doesn't it look

51

beautiful? *The Biggest Doll in the World*, and to think that our room will have it! Oh, Irma, I love you!"

Irma looked over her glasses and tried to smile at Judy, but her face hurt with the effort.

"Now, boys and girls," Miss Oglethorp said, "be sure to take the invitations home to your parents. It's going to be a lovely evening, and we want them all to come."

"We will, Miss Oglethorp," cried all of the children— all except Irma. Irma sat up very straight with her hands folded on her desk. The invitation, a bright orange rectangle, lay there in front of her, but she did not fold it up and put it into a book to take home, as the other children did.

In fact, when Irma left the room, the invitation was still lying on her desk, a very pretty piece of paper the color of ripe oranges. Irma had no use for it.

That evening Irma's father said to Uncle Arnold, "Well, the holiday toys are all unpacked. They'll be on display tomorrow for the first time."

"Don't forget to hire a Santa Claus with a real white beard," Uncle Arnold said. "You know how impossible it is to keep children from tweaking false beards."

"Yes, I know," Irma's father said, "but we won't need the Santa Claus until after Thanksgiving. There is plenty of time."

"But the dolls are there, Daddy?" asked Irma. "They are unpacked?"

"Yes, there's one of every kind out on display, Irma. The extra ones are waiting in the storeroom."

"*One of every kind*," thought Irma. "Oh, if only one is big enough!"

That evening Irma opened her bank and counted her money. There were a lot of dimes and nickels and pennies, but, when they were added up, they only came to four dollars and twenty-three cents. Irma was good at figures, but, just to make sure, she added her money five or six times. The sum was always the same, four dollars and twenty-three cents. No amount of adding could make it any larger. But Irma had other resources. In her tidy bureau drawer, under the neatly folded underwear and presentation handkerchiefs, was a birthday card from her Grandfather Wilson, on her mother's side of the family. The card said "To a Dear Little Girl" and it showed a small, fat girl with golden hair blowing out three candles on a cake. It had been a good many years since Grandpa Wilson had seen Irma, and she understood that he must think she had stopped growing when he saw her last. He wouldn't know how tall she was now, nor what a lot of trouble she was in.

But Grandpa Wilson had been generous. Inside the birthday card was folded a crisp new ten-dollar bill. Irma had been saving it, since her birthday in July, waiting until she saw something wonderful to buy with it. And now she was going to spend it for a doll that she really did not want. Irma sighed. Still it was good to know that she had fourteen dollars and twenty-three cents. If only this would be enough to get her out of trouble and set her straight with the world once again!

On the Saturday afternoon before the Harvest Home Carnival, Irma dressed carefully and put all of her money in her purse. The purse was heavy with so many nickels and dimes and pennies in it, and Irma had to put a rubber band around it to keep it from bursting open. She clutched it tightly against her side as she walked down through the park to Baumlein's Store. "I hope my purse will be empty when I come home again," Irma thought. "Should I try to carry the doll home with me? Or should I have it delivered?" She decided that she would have it delivered.

Crowds of people were going quickly along the street

in front of Baumlein's Store, and many others were going in and out of the revolving doors.

Irma paused before one of the show windows, and she saw that the window trimmer was removing a display of children's school clothing and was beginning to put in a toy display. A number of life-size dummies dressed in plaid and checkered dresses were pushed to one side of the window, while on the other side there were piles of games and space ships, monster-making sets and stuffed tigers. Yes, and there were dolls, but not very large ones.

Halfway between one display and another, the window was not very interesting to the passerby. Only the window trimmer and Irma seemed to be interested in what was going on.

The window trimmer was a young man with longish hair and sideburns. He wore a gray linen smock and had socks over his shoes so that he would not mar the carpeting of the display window. He was arranging a blue backdrop painted with large silver snowflakes to show off the holiday toys.

When he saw Irma, with her nose pressed to the glass, he winked at her and smiled. He seemed to be a nice young man. He held up one of the stuffed tigers for Irma to admire.

Irma shook her head. Then he held up one of the dolls. Irma nodded her head, at the same time holding up her arms to indicate that she wanted a much larger doll. This time the young man frowned and shook his head and went back to his work. She decided to go into the store.

# · 7 ·
# The Toy Department

Irma could remember a time when she had enjoyed getting into a revolving door and going around and around while timid people stood on the outside not daring to enter. But Irma had outgrown such foolishness, and today she didn't even go around one extra time.

Near the door and just behind the show window where the display was being changed stood several of the dummies waiting to be carted away. Irma noted with a flicker of interest that one of the dummies was about her size and that she had hair the color of ripe oranges.

"If only she were a doll!" thought Irma wistfully.

"What are you looking for, young lady?" asked a floorwalker who reminded Irma of Mr. Dillingham. He had the same haughty carriage and manner of looking down his nose at her.

"I'm looking for the toy department," Irma said.

"Take the elevator to the fifth floor and turn to your right," the floorwalker said.

Irma could remember a time when she had enjoyed riding up and down in an elevator and pushing all of the buttons for the different floors just for the pleasure of the ride.

But today she went straight to the fifth floor, got out, clutching her purse, and turned to her right. Ahead of her she saw the toy department, and her heart leaped with hope. It looked as if they had every kind of toy in the world.

Everything was beautifully new and shiny. Toy trains went around on shiny tracks, toy airplanes whizzed overhead. There were monster-making sets galore and stuffed tigers, elephants, monkeys, giraffes, and even little dogs that could be wound up and made to jump and bark.

Irma stopped wistfully beside the chemistry sets, but she knew that she would not have enough money left to buy one after she had bought the doll. So she went straight to the doll counter.

There were so many dolls that it made her head whirl. They were all smiling madly with very professional smiles. "Buy me! Buy me!" they seemed to say. "I'm just the one you want."

For a moment Irma was bewildered by all the smiling faces. She wondered if dolls ever frowned. They drank milk out of bottles and talked and cried and walked and probably even turned somersaults or danced, but they never seemed to frown. Perhaps those endless smiles were what made them seem stupid. Perhaps that was why Irma liked hamsters better.

"May I help you?" asked a lady who reminded Irma of Mrs. Dillingham. She had the same way of looking reproachful at the very moment when she was asking if she could be helpful.

"Yes," Irma said, looking over her glasses, "I should like to see the very largest doll you have, please."

"My dear little girl," said the saleslady patronizingly, "why do you want a *large* doll? The small ones do everything better than the large ones. Look at this adorable little doll now. She's called Darling Midget. She has three strings in her back. When you pull the first one, she says, 'Mama'; when you pull the second one, she says, 'Kiss me!'; when you pull the third one, she says, 'I love you.'"

"I'm sorry," Irma said, "but Darling Midget is not large enough."

"Well," said the saleslady crossly, "if it's only size and not quality that you want—"

"Size is very important to me," Irma said, taking off her glasses to polish them. "I want the Biggest Doll in the World."

"The Biggest Doll in the World!" cried the saleslady incredulously. "Well, I must say, you are asking for a great deal, little girl. But I'm sure that whatever it is you want, Baumlein's has it."

Irma did not wish to embarrass the lady by saying that

she knew Baumlein's was a good store because it was
founded by her great-grandfather, who was a man of integrity. So she just said, "Please show me the biggest
ones you have."

The saleslady began taking down dolls of all sizes.
Some were quite big—although not any bigger than
Beep, as far as that was concerned.

"No, it must be bigger," Irma kept saying. The saleslady lost all patience.

"Well," she said, "I hope that you can pay for it,
little girl, if you *do* find the biggest doll in the world."

Irma held out her bulging purse. "I have fourteen
dollars and twenty-three cents," she said.

The saleslady looked at Irma with more respect, but still she was skeptical. "*Only* fourteen dollars and twenty-three cents?" she cried. "Why, even Darling Midget costs twenty dollars, and the bigger they are, the more they cost."

"Dear me!" said Irma. "Haven't you any bargains?"

"Wait a minute," the saleslady said. "There's just a chance. Let me look in the supply room."

Irma waited as patiently as she could.

The saleslady was gone for some time, and when she came back she was carrying a tall, thin doll with very long legs. The doll was all made of cloth except for a wig of black hair and a pair of wire glasses. The black hair was parted in the middle and tied in two pigtails with red yarn. The large painted eyes of the doll seemed to be looking shyly over the tops of the wire glasses.

"Oh, dear!" thought Irma. "She looks like me!"

"Here you are, little girl," said the saleslady, "the largest doll we have. I'm sure she's just what you want, and she only costs fifteen dollars. A real bargain! You can ask your mama for the seventy-seven cents that you lack."

"Can she stand?" asked Irma.

The saleslady let the doll's feet touch the floor, but, as soon as she let go of her, the doll toppled over and fell on her face. The long, thin legs were only for show and not at all for standing.

"Well," said the saleslady, "you can't expect everything. She isn't made for standing."

61

"What *is* she made for?" Irma asked.

"She's a bed doll. The teen-agers like to put them on top of their beds along with all the little pillows and stuffed animals."

Irma looked at the bed doll as charitably as she could. Was there any possible way of using her? Would Judy or anyone else accept her as the Biggest Doll in the World, the doll with cerulean blue eyes and hair the color of ripe oranges? The answer, of course, was *no*. Still Irma kept looking at the doll, feeling so sorry for her—those glasses, those yarn-tied pigtails—no one would ever really love her! The teen-agers might put her on a bed among the many little pillows and stuffed animals, but they would only be laughing at her.

Irma kept silent for so long that the saleslady lost patience again.

"Well, little girl, do you want her or don't you want her?"

"I'm sorry," Irma said, "I don't—I can't use her. She isn't what I was looking for."

"Humpfh!" said the saleslady crossly. "I thought as much all of the time. Just looking, I suppose? That's what they all say, wasting my time."

"I'm sorry," Irma said again.

She turned around and went back to the elevator. It was full of people, and she could just squeeze in. Her glasses were so foggy that she could not see which button to press, but a kind, motherly-looking lady asked, "What floor, dear?"

"Main," said Irma in a small voice. The lady pressed the button for her. Everybody else seemed to be going to the main floor also. They pushed Irma out with them and left her floating and dizzy, not knowing where to go next or what to do. She thought vaguely of going to her father's office, but he would be busy and would not want to be bothered. Besides, she could never confess to him the terrible trouble that she had brought down on herself by her hasty words.

She moved slowly toward the main door. Although to others she may have looked like an ordinary little girl doing an errand for her mother, inside herself she was quite desperate.

When she came near the main door, Irma saw that the dummies from the old window display had not yet been carted away. There they stood, a group of pretty little girls, dressed for school. There was the one, just Irma's size, with hair the color of ripe oranges. Irma paused and looked at her, and she saw that her eyes were cerulean blue.

Before Irma stopped to think what a terrible thing she was doing, she lifted the dummy off its stand, and, with her arm around the dummy's waist, Irma walked it into the revolving door and out onto the street.

# · 8 ·
# A Walk in the Park

It was twilight out on the street and the lights were just coming on. Things looked strange at that time of day. The sky was still golden overhead, and the lights seemed unusually bright. Everything was a little confusing and unreal. Crowds of people were rushing along the street, doing last-minute errands before the stores closed and darkness settled down.

With her arm around the dummy Irma walked right into the crowd and nobody seemed to notice her, nobody that is, except a near-sighted old lady who said, "Dear child, has something happened to your little friend?"

"She hurt her foot," said Irma.

"How kind you are, dear, to help her walk!" the lady said.

"Yes, ma'am," said Irma in a very small voice.

At the corner Irma waited for the traffic sign to change, and then she hurried across the street in the midst of the crowd. The dummy was heavy, but Irma was too excited and frightened to notice this until she was safely at the edge of the park. Then she realized that she must stop for a moment and rest. She leaned the dummy up against the first support she found, and she stood in front of it so that people would not look at it and wonder.

Breathing heavily, Irma let her eyes wander up the support that she had found for the dummy, and she was shocked to see that it was the monument to Jacob Baumlein, a man of integrity. From his pedestal Great-grandfather Baumlein looked down at Irma and scowled.

That was the moment when Irma should have turned

around and marched the dummy back to Baumlein's Store. But she thought of the Carnival and the sign Peter had made and the invitation to the parents, and the picture of *Washington Crossing the Delaware* and the faces of Judy and all the other girls looking at her with love because she had brought the doll, or with disappointment because she hadn't.

"I'm just borrowing it," Irma said to the bust of Jacob Baumlein. "In three days I can bring it back again. I promise. Honestly, I promise."

Jacob Baumlein continued to frown. "But that's the way the artist made him," Irma said to herself. "He can't help frowning. He always does."

Nevertheless she was relieved when she could catch her breath enough to move the dummy into a quiet park path where bushes and trees offered a protective screen.

Irma found it easier to carry the dummy crossways with its head sticking out on one side of the path and its feet on the other. Even so, it was heavy and hard to manage. Whenever Irma heard someone coming, she set the dummy on its feet and stood in front of it, pretending to be talking to it. But nobody passed very close and nobody bothered to look twice at two little girls going home together in the twilight.

At one point, however, Irma had a real scare. She heard a cheery whistling and brisk footsteps coming behind her up the hill from town. Someone was coming along the very path that she and the dummy were using.

Hastily Irma pulled the dummy behind some bushes and crouched over it, so that neither of them could be seen from the path. The footsteps came closer; the whistling grew louder and more cheerful.

Peering between twigs and branches, Irma saw to her horror that the whistler on the path was a policeman. He looked very happy and relaxed as if he might be going home to dinner after a hard day's work. When he reached the spot where Irma was hiding, he stopped walking and whistling. He took off his helmet, stretched out his arms and drew a long breath. "Mmmmmmm!" he said as if he loved the smell of the drying leaves and the brisk autumn air.

Irma stopped breathing. Her glasses were so fogged that she could scarcely see, but this was no time to polish them. It seemed a very long time that the policeman stood there, but it must have been only a minute.

He began to whistle again, a different tune, but even more cheerful, and he walked on very jauntily with his helmet swinging by its strap from his hand.

Irma heard him going away and away. Finally he was gone and she began to breathe again. She yanked the dummy out onto the path and another terrible thing happened—its arm fell off. Before she picked up the curved pink arm that had slipped right out of the plaid sleeve, Irma stopped to polish her glasses.

"I must keep calm," Irma said to herself, "oh dear, I *must* keep calm."

When she could see again, she picked up the arm and

fitted it into the sleeve. "If I've broken her, what shall I do?" Irma thought. "I might as well call the policeman and give myself up right now."

But with a little trying, Irma found that the arm fitted into a socket at the dummy's shoulder. The arms were made to come off so that the window trimmer would find it easier to put the dummies into their clothes. All that was needed was to fit the arm into the socket and give it the proper twist to make it stay.

"Oh! If I ever get home!" Irma thought. She wasn't yet ready to face all of the problems that would arise when she *did* get home. Each moment that came was enough in itself.

So she toiled up the path with the dummy in her arms, and there was nothing more in her mind than reaching the top of the hill.

She was almost there, when, without a whistle or a heavy footfall, a boy suddenly crossed Irma's path. Irma stopped walking and set the dummy down. Next she put her arm around it and pretended that it was walking beside her. There was nothing else to do under the circumstances. She did not dare to look at the boy.

"Hurry up now, dear," she said to the dummy. "Don't drag your feet."

But there was something very familiar about the voice of the boy when he said, "Why, Irma Baumlein! You *do* have a big doll, don't you?"

Luke! Judy's brother, Luke!

Irma looked at him, and she saw that his eyes were

69

bugging with surprise. He was the only one who had not believed her.

"You *do* have the Biggest Doll in the World, don't you?" he cried. Irma's heart sank.

"Yes," she said in a small voice.

"Wait until I tell Judy!" Luke cried. "But what are you doing with her way out here?"

"I'm—I'm taking her for a walk."

"Gee! I thought she was so breakable."

"I'm trying to harden her up," Irma said, "so she can come to the Harvest Home Carnival."

"Man! Will Judy ever be relieved!" said Luke. "I almost talked her into thinking you didn't have a doll."

"You can see for yourself," said Irma sadly.

"Yes, I see. Can I help you walk her?" asked Luke.

"Oh, no, please," said Irma. "I'll get her home myself."

"Well, I really would go along and help you," Luke said, "but I'm late for supper already. Dad will be home —and I'd better scoot! See you at the Carnival, Irma!"

"See you at the Carnival, Luke," said Irma.

So now there was no one left in school who did not believe that she owned the Biggest Doll in the World. Irma should have been pleased to know that everything was turning out so well, but she was strangely depressed.

She managed to hide the dummy in the shrubbery at the side of the Baumlein mansion. Irma knew that the gardener would not come until Monday, and by that

time she hoped to have smuggled the dummy safely up to her room.

She stood under the mass of 1898 stones and pulled the bell. It was almost dark, but if Irma imagined that anyone had missed her, she was quite wrong.

She heard Mr. Dillingham coming along the hall with his measured tread, and when he opened the door he said as usual, "And how was school today, Miss Irma?"

"Just fine," said Irma. It seemed useless to remind him that this was Saturday. The world was all topsy-turvy anyway, and, if it was Friday to Mr. Dillingham and Saturday to Irma, it might be the Fourth of July to someone else.

Irma went up to her room, and there was BEEP, sitting in her little wicker chair and smiling with her tiny mouth and her two pearly teeth. A hamster would have been nicer, but still BEEP was becoming familiar now, and Irma looked at her with affection. There wasn't a doll like her among all of the Baumlein toys.

"Oh, what a day I've had!" Irma said.

"Don't tell me. I know all about it," BEEP seemed to say.

Irma was grateful.

# ·9·
# Another Restless Night

In spite of all the exercise she had taken, Irma's appetite was not very keen for dinner. She never had cared for roast lamb with mint sauce and spinach soufflé anyway.

"Clean your plate, dear," Aunt Julia said. "You'll never grow big if you don't eat."

"Big" was a word that Irma had recently grown to dislike.

"I don't care to be big," Irma said as politely as she could.

"You don't care a fig?" cried Aunt Julia in dismay. "Nephew, did you hear your daughter? I think she's being rude."

"No, no, Aunt Julia," said Irma's father loudly, "she just said that she did not care to be *big*. She meant no harm, I'm sure."

Irma ate her way doggedly through mashed potatoes and roast lamb and spinach soufflé. Nobody noticed that she left out the mint sauce.

"The oddest thing happened at the store today," said Irma's father to Great-uncle Arnold.

"Indeed?" said Uncle Arnold. "What was that?"

"One of the dummies was stolen."

"Stolen? Why would anyone want to steal a dummy?"

"I don't know, Uncle, but it's perfectly true. One of the dummies is missing. Apparently nothing else was taken. We've checked the jewelry department and the fur department and the TV department. Nothing else seems to be missing."

"That's very odd," said Uncle Arnold. "Usually shoplifters steal jewelry and furs before they steal dummies."

Irma tried to swallow a large bite of mashed potato, but it stuck in her throat and choked her. Mr. Dillingham, who stood behind her chair, had to slap her on the back to make her stop coughing.

"What have you done about it, Nephew?" asked Uncle Arnold. "I hope that you have notified the police."

"Not yet," Irma's father said. "Unfortunately, I am afraid there was some negligence involved. We have a new window trimmer, quite young and inexperienced. It seems that he left some of the dummies standing near the door of the store while he started to put toys into the window."

"He should have cleared away the dummies from the old display before he began to put in the new one."

"Exactly, Uncle. It was very careless of him to leave the dummies standing around with no one watching them."

Irma had a vision of the friendly face of the young window trimmer. He had smiled and winked at her.

In a still rather choked voice Irma heard herself saying: "Maybe it wasn't a thief. Maybe someone just borrowed the dummy for three days and will bring it back."

They all looked at her, and Irma felt herself blushing.

"Nonsense," Uncle Arnold said, "a thief is a thief."

"Clean your plate, dear," said Aunt Julia. "There's still a bit of mashed potato. And how about a little more mint sauce?"

"No, thank you, Aunt Julia," Irma said loudly.

"I'll tell you what," Uncle Arnold said. "Have the young man come up and see me tomorrow afternoon. Tell Mr. West, the floorwalker, to come with him. I'd like to impress on them the importance of taking care of the Baumlein stock. The sooner a young man realizes these things, the better it is for the store. What is the young window trimmer's name?"

"Bob Hickey," Irma's father said.

"Well, see that Bob Hickey comes up tomorrow, so that I can give him a little instruction."

Mr. Dillingham now removed the plates and brought in a large steamed pudding with brandy sauce.

"Excuse me," Irma said. "I'm not feeling very well. Do I have to eat dessert?"

"No, of course not," said her father. "Let me feel your head, Irma."

Irma stood by his chair and let him put his hand on her forehead.

"It's quite cool," he said. "I don't think you have a fever. Stick out your tongue, Irma."

Irma longed to throw herself into his arms and tell him everything. But with the Dillinghams and Great-uncle Arnold and Aunt Julia looking on, it seemed impossible.

"Your tongue is not coated. Does your head ache, Irma?"

"A little," Irma said. "I think I'm tired."

"What's the matter?" asked Aunt Julia. "No one ever tells me what is going on."

"She's tired," Irma's father shouted.

"Then why doesn't she go to bed?" asked Aunt Julia. Irma went around and dutifully kissed them all good night. Then she rushed to her room and began to undress for bed.

Sleeping was as difficult as eating. Beside her bed Irma had a little clock with a luminous dial. Ordinarily she did not watch the hours of the night creep by, but tonight she did.

At 12:30 Irma got up and put on her robe and slippers. The house was absolutely silent and very, very dark.

In the drawer of the night table by her bed Irma had a pocket flashlight that someone had given her. She had scarcely ever used it because it was not very good to read by. But now her reading days seemed to be over. She was living her adventures instead of reading them. She put the flashlight into the pocket of her robe and went cautiously to the bedroom door.

Very slowly she opened it, hoping it would not squeak. The hall was dark and quiet. In her soft slippers, Irma went silently down the stairs to the big front door. But before she unlatched it, she knew that she would have to find something to hold it open while she was outside. If it slammed shut she would be out in the cold for the rest of the night, or else she would have to ring for Mr. Dillingham. She could imagine Mr. Dillingham letting her in at one o'clock in the morning, looking down his nose at her in disapproval and saying, "And how was school today, Miss Irma?"

In the living room Irma found a small footstool and brought it to the front door. By the light of her pocket flash she could see the chain, the bolt and the latch that secured the front door against thieves who might try to come in from the outside and carry something away. In 1898, when the house was built, no one had ever thought to protect the Baumleins from a thief on the *inside* who might be trying to bring something *into* the house.

Very gently, so that it would not rattle, Irma unfastened the chain. The bolt was harder and she had to pull on it with all her might. Suddenly it shot back in its groove with a sharp click. Irma shivered with horror, and then she stood still listening. But the house was perfectly silent, except that far away, like the purr of a kitten, came the faint sound of Uncle Arnold's snoring.

The latch was easy, and with a blast of cold air the big front door swung open. Irma hastily shoved the footstool into place, so that after she was out the door would remain partly open. Then she dashed around the house and pulled the dummy out of the shrubbery.

"Trouble," she said to herself, "that's what I'm going to call her. Not Bertha Evangeline Esther Peebles, not Rosamonde or Gwendolyn or Kookidoodle—just Trouble. And don't lose your arm now, Trouble, for goodness sake!"

The dummy said not a word, but it resisted every effort of Irma to get it up the front steps and into the house. It was heavy, it was awkward, it made a bumping noise as Irma dragged it up the steps, and it stuck like a log in the small opening of the front door. Irma had to kick the footstool out of the way while she shoved the dummy across the threshold.

Once inside, Irma set the dummy up on its feet while she fastened the latch, the bolt and the chain on the front door. Then she hastily returned the footstool to the living room, and came back to the hall for the dummy. Of course the dummy's arm had fallen off, and Irma had to replace it before she could begin the long ascent of the stairs.

Halfway up the staircase was a landing with a deep window seat and a window overlooking the lawn. At night heavy crimson draperies were pulled across the window seat. Irma had often thought that it would be fun to hide in there behind the heavy curtains if one wanted to play hide-and-seek with friends. But, of course, Irma had no young friends in the house, so she had never tried hiding there. Tonight she thought of the landing as a place to rest on her way up to her room.

Taking a deep breath Irma started to drag Trouble up the first flight of stairs. Bump! bump! bump! went the dummy's feet on the steps of the stairway. It might have been well if Irma had taken more time and lifted the dummy more quietly over each step. But the more noise Trouble made, the more Irma hurried in order to get the ordeal over. Bump-bump-bump-bump-bump! went the dummy up the remaining steps to the landing.

Suddenly Irma heard a sound of heavy footsteps coming along the upper hall. She pulled Trouble hastily behind the draperies on the landing and stood very still. To Irma's ears the bump-bump-bump-bump-bump seemed still to be going on, but it was only her heart, and hopefully she was the only one who could hear it.

There was a moment of suspense and then Irma heard Mr. Dillingham's voice call out: "Who's there?"

Irma thought of squeaking like a mouse, or saying, "I AM A HAMSTER!" but she was afraid that Mr. Dillingham would recognize her voice. So she stood very still, clutching the dummy, and hoping that the bumping of her heart would not betray her.

"Who's there?" repeated Mr. Dillingham in a faltering voice.

Through a crack in the opening of the draperies, Irma could see Mr. Dillingham standing at the top of the flight of stairs with a flashlight in one hand and an umbrella in the other. He looked as frightened as Irma was.

"Who's there?" he demanded for the third time. There was no answer. If he had only flashed his light around the landing, he might have seen Irma's and the dummy's feet sticking out under the bottom of the drapery. Fortunately he did not do so.

After a long moment he said, "Humpf!" turned around, and went back the way he had come.

"What was it?" asked Mrs. Dillingham in the upper hall.

"Nothing, my dear," replied Mr. Dillingham. "Nothing at all. We can go back to bed."

Irma dared breathe again, but it seemed hours before she dared to move. She stood still so long that her joints congealed and she could scarcely move them. But she knew that she must not stand there until morning. Mr. Dillingham, coming down to lay the table for breakfast, would pull back the draperies and see her standing there, and say, "How was school today, Miss Irma?" And then he would see the dummy, and her troubles would be even greater than they were at present.

So finally Irma grasped the dummy firmly about its waist and slowly lifted it, step by step, up the remaining flight of stairs. She carried it cautiously along the hall to the door of her room. She had left her own door open a crack, so she was able to get the dummy into her room without further noise.

When she was safely in her own place, she drew a great sigh of relief. For a moment she rested. Then she lugged Trouble into her closet and set her up facing the door.

The dress was a bit mussed and Irma saw that she had screwed the dummy's arm in the wrong direction. One hand reached out forward and the other backward. But this was easily remedied. When Irma had both of the dummy's hands reaching forward, and the wrinkles in the dress smoothed out, she stood off and turned the flashlight full on the dummy's face.

There Trouble stood, just as Irma had always imagined, with cerulean eyes and hair the color of ripe oranges, the Biggest Doll in the World in Irma Baumlein's closet! Irma had a brief moment of pure happiness. Her dream had come true. Forgetting the worrisome past and not looking forward to the threatening future, Irma said to herself, *"I've done it!"*

She was very tired. She crawled into bed and fell at once to sleep.

# · 10 ·
# Quiet Sunday

Sunday was a quiet day in the Baumlein household. Mr. and Mrs. Dillingham took the day off, leaving cold cuts and a Russian salad in the refrigerator for the family luncheon. Aunt Julia went to church, although she heard very little and never could repeat the text of the sermon. Uncle Arnold stayed in his room, nursing his gout and worrying about the business of the store.

But Irma looked forward to Sunday because her father often took her on an excursion of some kind and they had a chance to be alone together. Irma thought that, if she could ever get him alone, she might—she just *might* —tell him of all the trouble she was in. It would be so good to let someone else share her burden and maybe advise her how she could become an honest child again. If her mother were only here! But that, of course, was out of the question.

At breakfast Mr. Baumlein was smiling more cheerfully than usual. "He's planned an excursion!" Irma thought. But, before she could ask him what it was, he said: "Irma, dear, I'm afraid I can't take you anywhere today. I have an appointment of the greatest importance this morning. If all goes as I hope it will, you may soon be very pleasantly surprised."

"Oh, Daddy!" Irma said. She did not know how to tell him that she wanted to be surprised *now*, not in some vague and uncertain *soon*. "How about this afternoon, Daddy?"

"I'm sorry," he said, "but this afternoon I must be with Uncle Arnold when he interviews the floorwalker and the window trimmer from the store."

"I see," said Irma, polishing her glasses.

"There was a theft at the store, you know."

"I know about the dummy," Irma said, "but I'm sure that someone only borrowed it—perhaps until after Tuesday."

"You don't understand these things, dear," Irma's father said.

"Oh, Daddy, yes, I do!" Irma said, and she would have gone ahead and told him, but just then Mr. Dillingham came in and said, "You're wanted on the telephone, sir. And if there is nothing further, sir, Mrs. Dillingham and I will be leaving at once for our day off."

"Certainly, Dillingham," said Irma's father. "Excuse me, Irma, I'll be back in time for lunch, dear." He kissed her on the forehead and went away to answer the telephone.

Irma ate another slice of cold toast with strawberry jam on it. She put the jam on very thick and she poured herself a cup of her father's coffee and drank it down without any sugar or cream. It tasted terrible. Then she cleared the dishes off the table and rinsed them in the pantry and stacked them neatly for the Live-in Couple to finish when they returned from their day off.

After that Irma went upstairs and made her bed and dusted all the furniture in her room. She hadn't remembered to bring her usual books home from the library on Friday night, and she now had nothing to read.

She went downstairs and looked in Uncle Arnold's library. None of the books had pictures and they appeared to be very solid and dull. The first title she noticed was *Crime and Punishment* by an author whose name looked as a sneeze might look if you tried to spell it. Irma sighed and went upstairs again.

Upstairs two pairs of eyes followed Irma around the room. BEEP from her wicker rocker and Trouble from the open closet gazed and gazed at her. Irma closed the closet door and put a bath towel over BEEP's head. Then she sat down and polished her glasses.

At 11:15 the doorbell rang. Irma nearly jumped out of her skin. Then she remembered that Mr. Dillingham was out and that she was probably the only person left in the house who could open the door.

She ran out into the hall, slid down the two banisters and arrived at the front door much more quickly than Mr. Dillingham ever did.

It was too early for Aunt Julia to be home from church, and much too early for the arrival of the men from the store.

Irma opened the door and there stood Judy and Luke. Judy's little dog stood beside them wagging his tail.

"Hi, Irma," said Judy.

"Well, *hi!*" said Irma in pleased surprise. Luke had a cardboard shoe box punched full of air holes under his arm, and Judy held out a bright orange invitation to the Harvest Home Carnival.

"Irma, you forgot your invitation. How will your mother and daddy know to come if they don't get the invitation? Lucky for you, I saw it on your desk Friday afternoon, and here it is."

"Oh, dear!" said Irma, "I didn't really want it—I—"

"Of course you could *tell* them," Judy said, "but I think a printed invitation is nicer, don't you, Irma?"

"Well, thank you very much, Judy. It's nice of you to come."

"Besides," continued Judy, "Luke told me about your doll and how you were taking it for a walk and everything, and I didn't want to wait all that long time until Tuesday to see it. So we just stopped by, and I hope you don't mind."

"Oh, no, I don't mind," Irma said. "In fact I'm very glad you came. Come right in." Judy's little dog had come up to sniff at Irma's shoes and now he looked up at her and wagged his tail and barked.

"He's saying hi," said Judy. "But don't worry, I won't let him come into your lovely house. Stay, Orbit!" Judy held up her finger at Orbit, and the little dog sat down obediently with his tongue out as if he were laughing.

"Will he wait for you?" Irma asked. "Won't he run away?"

"No. He'll be there when we come out."

The two children came into the big front hall and gazed around them.

"My, this is grand!" said Luke.

"Look, Irma," Judy said. "Luke has a surprise for you." She pointed toward the shoe box that Luke held under his arm.

"We thought you might like to see your hamster," said Luke. "I think he gets a little lonesome for you."

"The hamster!" cried Irma. "You mean—you mean, he still belongs to *me?*"

"Sure," said Luke. "We have a lot of them. This one is yours. We're just keeping him for you."

"Oh, my goodness! I never thought—I never thought I'd ever see him again."

Luke took the top off the shoe box, and there sat Orbit Two as big as you please. In one corner of the box he had made a nest of torn paper, and sunflower seeds were scattered all around.

"Oh, the darling! The darling, darling thing!" cried Irma.

"Take him out," said Luke. "I think he remembers you."

Irma took the hamster out of his box. Oh, that delicious soft and furry feeling of something alive and friendly in her hand! He looked at Irma with his beady eyes and then he ran up her arm to her shoulder and sat there nibbling at the red wool tie on her pigtail.

"Oh, I love him," Irma said. "But, you know, they won't let me keep him."

"I know," Luke said, "this is just a visit, so he won't forget you."

"And now," said Judy, "could we see the doll?"

"Oh, yes," said Irma, "come up to my room. She's up there."

"I know," said Judy, "in your closet."

Irma put the hamster back in his box, and as they went upstairs, she could feel him bumping around inside it. Just the feel of him made her terribly happy.

When they reached her room, Judy rushed around looking at everything.

"Oh, what a lovely room! Do you sleep in it *all* alone? No sisters to share the bed? What a darling dressing table! And look, Luke, she's got a bathroom all to herself. She doesn't have to stand in line to get washed in the morning before school."

Judy whisked the bath towel off BEEP's head. "Oh, she's adorable!" she cried. "Look at those eyes! Only they aren't cerulious blue—and she's not so very, awfully big, is she?"

"No, no," Irma said, "that's BEEP—I mean Bertha Evangeline Esther Peebles. She belonged to my Great-aunt Julia. She's not the one."

"I'll say she isn't," said Luke. "The one I saw in the park is as big as Irma."

Irma drew a long breath, and then she opened the closet door.

"Well, there she is," she said. Trouble stood there with her hands outstretched. She smiled and her eyes were cerulean blue, her hair the color of ripe oranges. Surely no one could ask for more.

Judy stood back and looked at her. At last she said,

"She's awfully nice, she really is. I never saw one so big before. My goodness! She reminds me of someone I've seen somewhere."

"You've imagined her so often," Luke said, "that's why she looks familiar to you."

"Yes, that must be it," Judy said slowly.

"Didn't I tell you?" said Luke. "Did you ever see a bigger one?"

"No, I never did," Judy said. She continued to gaze at the Biggest Doll in the World with a puzzled look on her face. "Somewhere I've seen—"

"How could you?" protested Luke. "I guess there isn't another doll in the world this big."

"It's just—it's just that she reminds me of something— somewhere—"

"How are you going to get her down to the school?" asked Luke practically.

"I don't know yet," Irma said. "That's one of my problems."

"We'll come and help you," Luke said, "won't we, Judy?" Irma thought very swiftly of how it could be done. "If you could come about six-thirty on Tuesday. It's dark then and Mrs. Dillingham will be in the kitchen and Mr. Dillingham will be serving dessert, and often I don't eat dessert if it is suet pudding or something—no one makes me. And then I could let her down out of the window and you could be there to catch her and we could take turns carrying her over to the school—"

Judy looked at Irma in surprise. "But I thought you asked your mother. Doesn't she know?"

"My mother doesn't know," Irma said, and that was true anyway.

"Then maybe we shouldn't take her," said Luke.

"Oh, Luke!" cried Judy, "we've got to take her. Everyone's counting on it, and it's printed on the invitations and everything. It's terribly important, and we'll be awfully careful of her."

"Well, where do you want us to meet you then?" asked Luke.

"You see this window?" Irma said. "If I can get a rope, I'll let her down out of the window. Look outside now and see those bushes down below? That's where she'll be on Tuesday evening about six-thirty."

"Okay!" said Luke. "We'll be there. But in the meantime, maybe you'd better tell your mother."

"I'll try," said Irma.

"Well, we must go," Judy said. "Mother said we were only to stay a very few minutes. But listen, Irma, could you bring BEEP too on Tuesday evening? I really like her better than the big one. We could make a sign and say she was the Oldest Doll in the World."

"No one would believe that," said Luke. "She looks old all right, but nobody would believe she was the oldest."

"But she's simply darling!" Judy said, giving BEEP a kiss on her tiny mouth with the two pearly teeth.

"Don't be silly," Luke said. "Come on now, Judy. We've got to go."

After they had gone the house seemed quieter than ever. If only they could have left the hamster!

Irma sat down at the little writing desk that had belonged to some vanished second-cousin-twice-removed who had once occupied this room. She took out a sheet of writing paper and started a letter.

*Dear Mother:* Irma wrote, *I'm in a lot of trouble and I wish you were here. I told a lie and I stole a dummy but I'm going to return it after Tuesday and I wish you were here—I wish you were here—I wish you were here —Love, Irma.*

But when she read it over, the letter seemed impossible. Irma crumpled it up in a ball and dropped it into the wastepaper basket. She put the orange-colored invitation to the Harvest Home Carnival into the wastebasket also. Her father would be too busy to come and her mother was far away, and anyway she did not want either one of them to come and see how badly she had got herself into trouble.

# · II ·

# The Window Trimmer Again

In the afternoon, when the doorbell rang, Irma knew it could only be Bob Hickey and Mr. West coming from the store to be lectured by Uncle Arnold. She peeped over the banister and saw her father letting them in the front door.

"How are you?" Irma's father said in a cheery voice. "It's a lovely day, isn't it?" Irma knew that he was trying to be kind, but Mr. West looked very stern and Bob Hickey looked frightened.

"This is a most unfortunate thing, Mr. Baumlein, sir," said Mr. West. "To think of our having a dummy stolen, sir, right under our noses, sir, so to speak. A most unfortunate thing! Bob Hickey was very greatly at fault for leaving the dummies there while changing the window display. He should certainly have carted off the dummies before he began to put in the toys. Am I not correct, Mr. Hickey?"

"You are correct, sir," said Bob Hickey in a low,

repentant voice. Irma could see that he had already been scolded enough even before Uncle Arnold got at him.

"Well, come this way please," Irma's father said. "I am sure that Mr. Hickey meant no harm. Mr. Arnold Baumlein only wishes to speak to him about the importance of caring for the Baumlein stock at all times as if it were his own."

"Yes, sir! Indeed, sir!" Mr. West said. Their voices faded out as they went into Uncle Arnold's study and closed the door behind them.

"If I could only tell them that it will be all right after Tuesday!" Irma said to herself. He looked such a nice young man and he had winked and smiled at her and held up a tiger and a doll to show her. Today all of the smiles and winks had been scolded out of him, and it was entirely her fault.

She went back into her room. The closet door was still open, and Trouble still stood there beaming as she had beamed at Judy a few hours before. It was funny that Judy hadn't really liked Trouble. She had liked BEEP better. Irma closed the closet door and turned around to look at BEEP.

BEEP was sitting just as Judy had left her after Judy had given her a kiss. The old doll's arm was upraised and she seemed to be pointing at something. Irma's eyes followed the pointing hand and there on the dressing table lay her bulging purse with a rubber band around it to hold in the fourteen dollars and twenty-three cents.

*Money!* Oh, dear, that's what a store was all about. The store bought dolls at wholesale prices, and then people paid regular prices to buy the dolls, and the extra money between the wholesale and the retail price went to Uncle Arnold and kept the store running and paid salaries for Mr. West and Bob Hickey. Irma really did not care very much about money, so long as she could buy bubble gum and hamster food (if she *had* a hamster). But now she saw that it was very important, even to pleasant people like Bob Hickey. He probably had an aged mother who sat in a wheelchair and maybe he had ten little brothers and sisters who would starve if he did not bring home his wages from Baumlein's every week. She saw it all so clearly. Irma had to take off her glasses and polish them when she had imagined this.

"I will give my money to Bob Hickey," Irma said to herself. "Maybe that will make up to him for all the scoldings he is getting."

But how was she going to give Bob Hickey her money without arousing everyone's suspicions? After Tuesday she would return the dummy and explain everything. But, in the meantime, she could not bear the thought of Bob Hickey and his aged mother in her wheelchair and the ten hungry brothers and sisters suffering needlessly on her account.

Above the fancy portico that overhung the Baumleins' big front door there was a little balcony. It would have been a good place for Rapunzel, Rapunzel to let down her long hair, or for Juliet to sit while Romeo played the guitar to her from down below. Irma had often imagined romantic uses for the balcony, but now it seemed to her that it might serve a practical purpose.

Irma put on her coat and cap because she did not know how long she might have to wait in the chilly air. She took her purse with fourteen dollars and twenty-three cents in it, and she went along the upstairs hall to the front of the house. A round, stained-glass window overlooked the balcony above the portico. There was no door. Evidently the house had not been planned with Rapunzel or Juliet or Irma in mind. The balcony was just another excuse for the builder to put more fancy lace woodwork on his gingerbread house.

But Irma did not give up easily. She saw that there was a latch on the side of the stained-glass window that could be opened. At least, it could be opened after Irma had got a little butter from the pantry and rubbed it on the latch to lubricate it. With a creaky sound the round window swung outward, and Irma found that she could just squeeze through the opening and get herself onto the balcony. It was terribly untidy, full of dried leaves and the dust of years.

Irma felt like doing good today and she seriously considered getting a broom and giving the balcony a smart clean-up. But she was afraid that, if she did, she might miss Bob Hickey's departure, and that, after all, was the reason she had climbed out here. So she sat down patiently to wait.

The sparrows in the neighboring trees were quite upset to see someone sitting on the dirty floor of the Baum-lein balcony after so many years. They had considered the balcony a part of their own property, and now they fluttered around and scolded and fussed. But Irma liked birds almost as much as she liked hamsters, and gradually the sparrows grew used to her and went back to their own affairs. Irma made a mental note to bring some crumbs or hamster seed the next time she used the balcony. She even thought that she might tame a bird and teach it tricks and let it live in the cage from the attic. But no, she decided, birds were meant to be free in the trees. She didn't want one of them shut up in a fancy cage all alone and away from its fellows.

At last there was a noise of departure from the great front door beneath the balcony and the portico.

Irma heard her father's kindly voice saying, "Well, after all, it was only a dummy. It might have been a mink coat or an expensive piece of jewelry."

"No! No!" said Mr. West's voice. "The value of the theft is not important. The main thing is that we take care of Baumlein's stock. Bob Hickey was at fault in this."

"Don't be too hard on him," Irma's father said.

Irma knelt by the balcony railing and peered over. She saw Mr. West come out of the house, winding his muffler about his neck and settling his hat upon his head. With dignity and pride he walked away.

"Oh, *what* have they done to Bob Hickey?" worried Irma. She could imagine all sorts of terrible things.

But apparently Uncle Arnold had just detained Bob for a few more words of wisdom. In about ten minutes the door opened again, and without any conversation, Bob Hickey came hastily out.

As soon as Irma saw him emerge beyond the portico she stood up and hurled her purse at him. There it went, her precious fourteen dollars and twenty-three cents, but it was the best she could do for him at the moment.

It hit him squarely on the head (Irma had not intended *that*), and the purse broke open, scattering nickels, dimes and pennies like a flurry of solid snowflakes all about him. The ten-dollar bill floated gracefully to the ground like a tired autumn leaf.

Bob Hickey let out a frightened yelp and gazed wildly about him. Irma had to duck down so that he would not see her. But then, instead of picking up the money, as Irma had hoped he would be sensible enough to do, he took to his heels and ran as fast as he could go down all the many stone steps and away into the park.

"Oh, dear!" Irma said to herself. "None of my good ideas seem to work—only my bad ones. And now what's going to become of the mother in the wheelchair and all the hungry brothers and sisters?"

It had been a gloomy Sunday.

Irma crawled in the window and closed it carefully. Then she went outdoors and picked up the ten-dollar bill and the dimes and nickels and pennies that lay scattered about the lawn. One penny she never did find, so now she had fourteen dollars and twenty-two cents and there was a big hole in the side of her purse.

When she came back to her room, there sat BEEP smiling at her.

"You made me do it," Irma said crossly. "You pointed at the purse and made me think of it."

But then Irma was sorry, for all of us make mistakes.

So she took BEEP out of her chair and held her. "You are a good doll," Irma said, "even if I don't really care for dolls, and you don't smell as much of mothballs as you did last week. Maybe I could get to like you in time."

BEEP's eyes clicked open and shut and her joints creaked, but she made Irma feel more comfortable.

# · 12 ·

# Do Whatever You Like, Irma

Before she left for school on Monday morning Irma put Trouble far back in the dark part of her closet and draped an old coat over her. Even if Mrs. Dillingham came up to clean the room, Irma felt that she would not get far enough back in the closet to discover the dummy.

Monday and Tuesday went by for Irma like very long, bad dreams. Everybody at school loved her, and that, of course, was gratifying. Judy had told everyone that she had seen the doll and that it really was as big as Irma said. She told them about BEEP too, and how old she was.

"Couldn't we have one of the oldest dolls in the world on display, too, Miss Oglethorp?" Judy asked.

"I think it would be very nice," Miss Oglethorp said, "that is, if Irma is willing."

"Oh, yes," Irma said. At least BEEP was genuine and there was nothing disgraceful to be discovered in her past.

So Peter made another sign that said:

Everyone was very excited. Most of Tuesday afternoon was spent in arranging their space in the big auditorium. The folding chairs had been taken out to clear the floor, and each grade had its own particular space. The children of that grade could do whatever they wished with that space.

Miss Oglethorp's room had tables for exhibits where Henry could display his model airplanes, and Peter could display his drawings, and Mary could put the show cage for her Siamese cat. It turned out that other children in the room had hobbies also. Jim brought a

collection of rocks that he had gathered in the desert, and Gwen had a collection of buttons that had mostly come out of her grandmother's button bag. Otto collected old coins, and Billy collected stamps.

Irma was much interested in these collections, and she would have had a good time, except that in the very center of the exhibit was a large screen which was reserved for *The Biggest Doll in the World* and *One of the Oldest Dolls in the World*, both belonging to Irma Baumlein. There was no way that Irma could forget it.

"I think that we could charge ten cents instead of five cents, now that we are going to have two dolls," Judy said. "It would be that much more for the library fund."

Everybody agreed with Judy except Irma who did not say anything at all.

"Miss Oglethorp, my brother Luke and I are going up to Irma's house and help her bring her dolls right after dinner," Judy said.

"And don't forget your little dog!" several children cried.

"Certainly not!" said Judy. It had been agreed that Judy would put Orbit through his tricks during the program up on the big stage at the end of the auditorium. Rodney would do his card tricks there just before Judy performed with her little dog. It would be part of the general program.

"I think we're going to have the best, the very best show of any of the grades," Mary said. "I'm sure we'll win the picture for our room."

"Well, don't count on it in advance," Miss Oglethorp said. "Just try to do your best, each one of you, and whatever the judges decide, I'm sure we'll all be satisfied."

"I know, Miss Oglethorp," Mary said, "but with Judy's little dog and Irma's dolls, I don't see how we can lose."

"If only everything goes just right!" Irma said to herself. She could not help feeling anxious. She had been lucky enough to find a coil of rope in the attic, but she didn't know whether she could lower the dummy successfully out of her window without attracting attention or not. Many perils lay ahead of her.

Just before dinner on Tuesday evening Irma met her father in the lower hallway. He was getting his coat and hat out of the hall closet.

"Irma, darling," her father said, "I won't be here for dinner tonight. Be a good girl and mind Aunt Julia, and something very nice is bound to happen."

Irma could not think of anything nice that could possibly happen to her under the present circumstances. But her father's absence meant one less threat to her desperate plans for the evening. She gave him a kiss, hardly noticing how pleased and happy he looked. It was nice that someone in her family could be happy anyway.

Dinner was unusually silent. Uncle Arnold did not have anyone to ask about the store, and neither he nor Irma felt like shouting to Aunt Julia. Irma realized that there were two subjects she must discuss with Aunt Julia before the meal was over, but she did not know how to begin. She must tell Aunt Julia that she was going out after dinner and she must ask Aunt Julia's permission to take BEEP with her. If she could have spoken in a low voice, it might have been easy. But to start shouting all this in the midst of a silent dinner was very difficult. And the time was ticking on toward 6:30.

Irma ate her way through a lot of roast beef and cauliflower and mashed potatoes.

"What's for dessert, Dillingham?" Uncle Arnold asked. His voice made Irma jump. Oh! What a relief to hear someone speak!

"Tapioca pudding and pound cake, sir," said Mr. Dillingham.

"I don't want it," Uncle Arnold said. "Help me to my room, please, Dillingham."

"Yes, indeed, sir!"

With a sigh of relief, Irma saw them depart. She plucked up all her courage, and folding her napkin neatly, she went quite close to Aunt Julia.

"I don't care for any dessert either, Aunt Julia," she said.

"What! No ice cream and cake?" said Aunt Julia.

"It's tapioca pudding, Aunt Julia."

"How's that, dear?"

"Aunt Julia, I have to go out to a meeting at school tonight."

"Night school?" Aunt Julia said. "But you go in the

daytime, dear. How *was* school today, by the way?"

"Just fine," Irma said, "but, Aunt Julia, this is the Harvest Home—"

"I know you are excited about your new home, dear. Is there anything I can do?"

"Could I take Bertha Evangeline Esther Peebles, Aunt Julia?"

"You mean Bertha Evangeline Esther Peebles, dear?"

"Yes, Aunt Julia."

"Certainly, Irma, she's yours now. Do whatever you like."

Irma gave Aunt Julia a kiss. She really did love her, although it was almost impossible to talk sensibly with her. There were a number of gaps in their understanding of each other, but Irma took her last words as final. *Do whatever you like.*

Irma rushed up to her room and shut the door. Then she dragged Trouble out of the closet and tied the rope around her waist. She opened the window and looked out. There were Judy and Luke already waiting on the lawn below. Their faces looked round and pale in the reflected light from the open window.

"Okay," Luke said. "Lower away."

Irma hoisted Trouble over the window sill and began to lower her gently inch by inch down the side of the house. When the dummy was about halfway down, there came a knock on Irma's door.

"Oh, goodness!" Irma said to herself. "What next?"

She let go of the rope and Trouble went banging down the rest of the way and fell into a heap of bushes and reaching arms.

Irma turned from the open window just in time to see Mrs. Dillingham coming in her door with a tray of food.

"Madame said you did not like tapioca pudding, Miss Irma. So she's sent you a dish of ice cream instead."

"Oh, thank you! Thank you!" Irma cried. "Oh, thank you, Mrs. Dillingham." She couldn't think of another thing to say, and she might have gone on saying thank you indefinitely, but Mrs. Dillingham had seen the open window.

"Miss Irma, it's far too chilly tonight to have your

windows open. What in the world were you doing with an open window?"

"I—I felt a little faint," Irma said, and that was certainly the truth for at the moment she felt very, very faint.

"Well, close it at once, my child. Shall I stay while you eat your ice cream?"

"Oh, no! Thank you! Thank you! It may take me quite a long time to eat it. I'll leave the tray in the hall, Mrs. Dillingham."

"Very well," Mrs. Dillingham said in a huffy voice and took herself off.

Irma closed the window. Then she scraped the delicious-looking ice cream into the bowl in the bathroom and flushed it neatly away. Then she put on her coat and cap, took up BEEP under one arm and the little wicker chair under the other, and when the hall was quiet and deserted, she hurried downstairs and let herself out the front door. How she was to get back in again later she hadn't a notion, but after all, she couldn't possibly plan for everything at once.

Luke and Judy followed by Orbit came around the house, carrying the dummy. They met Irma at the front steps.

"Oh, Irma," Judy whispered. "Why did you let her down so fast? Something perfectly terrible has happened!"

"It's awful," Luke said. "Your mother will never forgive us."

Irma gave a groan. Her glasses needed polishing very badly, but her hands were full and she couldn't take time for polishing now. She went blindly down the stone steps.

"What?" she asked. "What other terrible thing could possibly happen?"

"The doll is broken," Judy said. "The Biggest Doll in the World! The thing you love the best! Irma, when she fell down, her arm broke off."

"Let me see," said Irma. She looked over the tops of her foggy glasses, and Judy held up a beautiful curved pink arm.

In the midst of her anxieties, Irma laughed. Trouble had played her usual trick on them.

"It's all right," Irma said. "She does that. Bring the arm along, and let's get to school as fast as we can."

"The doll will be safe after we get to school anyway," Luke said. "Nobody will dare to steal her, because our father has been assigned to guard the exhibits."

"Your father?" faltered Irma.

"Yes, didn't you know?" asked Judy. "Our father is a policeman. He's the best man on the force—or anyway *we* think so. He's going to guard our school tonight."

"That's why we know that everything will be safe," said Luke.

"Oh!" said Irma.

# · 13 ·
# Harvest Home

The auditorium of the Washington School was buzzing with excitement. The parents had not yet begun to arrive, but all of the children and teachers were there, putting last touches on booths or exhibits. There were orange and yellow paper streamers draped around the walls, and on the stage were cornstalk teepees and pumpkins and bunches of autumn leaves. Nothing looked like everyday. It was all magical, as if some wizard had waved a wand and made an enchanted place out of the auditorium, where the principal usually made announcements and the sixth-graders sang a little off-key. Tonight the teachers wore pretty dresses and even the boys and girls looked different, more combed and polished and shiny.

Irma had not thought to change into her best dress or to tie blue yarn strings on her pigtails instead of red ones. She looked at the animated scene with admiration as well as dismay. She hadn't an idea what to do next. But Luke took charge of everything.

"Take off your coat and put it over the doll's head," he said. "We don't want anyone to see her now, or they might not pay ten cents to go in and see her later. If we go around the side of the auditorium to your grade's place and put her right behind the screen, no one will see her."

"BEEP, too," Judy said. "I'll cover her with my coat, so she will be a surprise too."

"Come along," Luke said. Irma followed him obediently. It was nice to have somebody else making the plans. Actually Luke belonged to the next higher grade, but he had become so interested in helping Judy and Irma with the dolls that he really enjoyed telling everybody what to do. When they arrived safely at Miss Oglethorp's booth, the other children crowded around to see what they had brought.

"Just the ones in our grade may see," said Judy. "No one else may until they pay their dimes."

Luke set the dummy up behind the screen, and Irma screwed her arm in place and smoothed out her dress. Judy was busy arranging BEEP in her little chair. The girls who had heard so much about Irma's doll came crowding around. "Oh!" they said. "Oh! *Ah!* Oh!"

"She does have cerulean eyes," said Miss Oglethorp.

"And hair the color of ripe oranges!" cried Mary.

Irma was silent, trying to resist a great feeling of pride. It would not do to begin feeling proud at the very moment when her crime was most likely to be discovered.

"What's her name?" Luke demanded. "Do you just call her Doll? Or what?"

Irma thought rapidly. They wouldn't understand if she told them that the dummy's name was Trouble.

"You may call her Troubella," said Irma, looking over her glasses.

"Troubella," all the girls said. "What a lovely name! We never heard it before."

"I think it's Spanish," Irma said vaguely.

"You know," Judy said, "now that I see her in this bright light, I can think what she reminds me of."

"What does she remind you of?" asked Mary, who had come up to look over Judy's shoulder at the Biggest Doll in the World.

"She reminds me a little—just a little teeny bit—of one of the dummies in Baumlein's window," Judy said.

"Don't be silly!" cried Mary, and all the girls said, "Oh, Judy! How can you? The Biggest Doll in the World, and she reminds you of a dummy."

"Goodness, Judy!" Luke said. "You ought to be able to tell a doll from a dummy any day!"

"It's just her size, I guess," Judy said. "Of course, this one is a doll and much prettier than any dummy. I don't know how I got such a dumb idea."

"A dummy idea," laughed Luke.

Irma did not say anything, but she breathed a long sigh. Later, when she happened to look around, she saw that a policeman was standing just outside the booth, smiling at them. He was the very policeman she had seen in the park the day she took the dummy from the store.

"Now!" Irma thought. "This is the end of it all!"

But just then Judy also saw the policeman. "Daddy, you can't come in yet!" she cried. "You'll have to wait until everything's ready. Then you'll have to pay a dime to see the dolls, just as all the other parents do."

Officer Miller laughed. "Hey!" he said, "don't I get to see what I am guarding?"

"No! No!" the other children shouted.

"Not until the other parents come and you pay to get in."

"It's all for the good of the library fund," Judy cried, "and we want to win the picture for our room, you know, Daddy."

"How about that, Irma?" laughed Judy's father. "Do I have to wait and pay a dime to see these famous dolls I've been hearing so much about?"

"I guess you do," said Irma in a small voice. Officer Miller looked so nice, so jolly, so much fun; and nobody else was afraid of him. Irma took off her glasses and polished them with her handkerchief.

Before long the mothers and fathers and the older and younger brothers and sisters began to arrive for the Harvest Home. There was a lot of noise of talking and laughing and of people moving around. Irma's head whirled.

Soon people began to come and pay their dimes to go in and see the doll exhibit. Peter and Henry sat at the table nearest the screen, and they collected the dimes and put them in an empty egg carton, where they could easily make change.

"Oh!" said all the little sisters and brothers. "Oh! *Ah!* Oh!" and the mothers and fathers said, "So that's the Biggest Doll in the World! Well! Well!"

Judy and Mary stood by and said, "Her name is Troubella. It's a Spanish name. And the other one is Bertha Evangeline Esther Peebles. Aren't they wonderful?" Irma did not have to do a thing but hover nervously wondering how soon the evening would be over.

Matthew, Mark and John came by, not because they were interested in dolls, but because they had heard Judy and Luke talking so much about Irma Baumlein's big one. And then Mrs. Miller and Patty came. The tiny baby was fast asleep at home with a sitter.

Judy was so pleased to see them, and the little dog frisked and barked. Patty tried to take some of Jim's rocks off the table and put them in her mouth, and then she tried to put one of Gwen's buttons up her nose, and finally she tried to let Mary's cat out of the cage. But Judy wasn't cross with her. "No, no, darling," she kept saying, "mustn't touch, just look at all the pretty pretties."

Mrs. Miller came and took Irma's chin in her hand and tilted up her face to look at her. "My! My!" she said. "How nice to see you, Irma. And are you having a good time, dear?"

"Yes, thank you," Irma said, looking shyly over the tops of her glasses. And she thought how nice, *how nice* it was to have Judy's mother notice her.

"Come on now, Mama," Judy said, "and pay your dime and one for Patty, and come in and see Irma's dolls. And, Patty, mustn't touch, dear, mustn't touch."

"Where's Daddy?" asked Luke.

"Oh, he's busy just now," Mrs. Miller said, "there are so many things to guard. He told us not to wait for him. He'll be here very soon. He wants to see Irma's dolls too."

"We wouldn't let him in earlier because we weren't ready to take his dime," Judy said. "Come on now, Mama, come and look!"

When they came out again Mrs. Miller put her arm around Irma's shoulder.

"Why, Irma, they're lovely dolls," she said. "I never saw such a big one before in my life."

"That's because it's the Biggest Doll in the World," said Luke.

"But I like the old one best," Mrs. Miller said. "My grandma used to have one quite a bit like it, but she wouldn't let me touch it for fear I would break it."

"Maybe you were like Patty, Mama," Judy said, hanging onto her mother's arm. "Maybe you wanted to handle everything and put things in your mouth."

"Maybe I was," said Mrs. Miller. They went away laughing together to look at the other booths.

It was nice to see the children greeting their mothers and fathers when they came. Everyone seemed so happy. Irma couldn't help feeling a little envious as she watched them take their parents up to meet Miss Oglethorp.

Sometimes Miss Oglethorp already knew the parents; sometimes she seemed so glad to meet the ones she didn't know. "My! How Henry's spelling has improved since school started, Mrs. Nugent." "I think that we can be proud of Mary now, Mr. Hogan. She's really digging into that arithmetic. It's not half as bad as she thought, is it, Mary?"

"It's still pretty bad, Miss Oglethorp," Mary said, "but I'm catching on to it."

"We're proud of Mary," Mrs. Hogan said.

After her parents had gone on by, Mary said, "When are *your* parents coming, Irma?"

"They may be late," said Irma cautiously.

Irma decided that she would go out to the door for a few minutes and get a breath of fresh air. Her head had begun to ache and all of that roast beef and cauliflower and mashed potatoes that she hadn't wanted to eat for dinner felt very tipsy-topsy in her stomach.

People were still coming in and going out of the auditorium door. Irma stepped outside and leaned up against a pillar and closed her eyes. The night air was cool and pleasant on her forehead. Presently she felt better.

"Oh, well!" she said, and went back in again.

Suddenly she saw just ahead of her a jaunty-looking young man with a pretty girl on his arm. There were no old ladies in wheel chairs, no starving brothers and sisters, only a pretty girl, and—yes, it was—*Bob Hickey!*

He looked at Irma and smiled and winked. He was much happier than he had looked on Sunday, and Irma saw that he did not recognize her at all.

Irma's stomach began feeling very odd again. She turned around and made for the door, but one of the teachers was just closing it.

"You can't go out now," the teacher said. "The program is just about to begin. You'll miss the best part if you leave now, dear. Everyone's staying until the program's over."

A crowd of people moving toward the stage at the far end of the long room caught Irma up with them and swept her along. There was no way to disentangle herself. In a few moments Irma found herself standing just below the platform, squeezed in like a hot dog surrounded by buns, and not a drop of mustard to help her slip out.

The principal was standing just above her, clearing his throat.

"Ladies and gentlemen, boys and girls, we welcome you to Washington School tonight. We welcome you to the Harvest Home Carnival. We hope that you are enjoying yourselves."

Everyone clapped to show how much they were enjoying themselves. And then the program began.

# · 14 ·
# Stop the Program

Wedged in tight, Irma could hardly move, but she looked all around her and Bob Hickey was not in sight. Irma could see belt buckles and coattails and ladies' backs, and here and there the top of a small child's head. The view was not extensive. She could only hope that Bob Hickey and the pretty young lady cared so little for dolls that they would not pay twenty cents to see the Biggest one.

By tipping her head back, Irma could look straight up and see what was going on above her on the stage. The sixth-graders all came out now with a loud noise of tramping feet, and sang "Believe Me, If All Those Endearing Young Charms." Irma was no judge of music, but the sixth-graders seemed off-key as usual, and Irma felt sure that they would not win. With a loud noise of tramping feet, they all went away again, and a drummer came to replace them. He was very loud too, and when he crashed the cymbals on the side of his drum, Irma would have jumped right out of her skin except that she was packed in so tightly that she couldn't.

After the drummer came a P.T.A. lady in a blue lace dress who recited a poem called "When Lilacs Last in the Dooryard Bloom'd." It was very long with lots about stars and shades of night and birds singing in swamps and coffins. It was mournful enough to suit Irma's mood, and she felt that she might have enjoyed it if she had had more room for breathing. However, before it was over, the crowd began to move a little and give Irma more room. It seemed to Irma that perhaps the program was not going off very well, especially since there was nowhere to sit.

But after the lady in blue lace things began to improve. Rodney was next with his card tricks, and Irma was proud to see that he did not drop any cards and that most of his tricks succeeded in mystifying the audience. He got a good round of applause, and Irma thought, "He's the best one yet, but wait until they see Judy and Orbit."

Judy had changed into a clown costume, and Orbit had a red and white ruffle around his neck. They looked interesting, and the audience began to move in close again.

Irma thought how frightened she would have been to stand up there on the platform and speak to so many people. But Judy was quite calm and spoke in a loud clear voice.

"Ladies and gentlemen and boys and girls," Judy said

(just as the principal had said, but ever so much better, Irma thought). "I want to introduce to you my educated dog. His name is Orbit, and perhaps you can guess why." At the sound of his name, Orbit began turning around and around trying to catch his tail. Everybody laughed, and after the endearing young charms and the lilacs, this was a great relief. Then Judy had Orbit stand on his hind legs and shake hands and beg and jump over a stick. Then to rest Orbit's legs Judy had him roll over and play dead. When he jumped up, barking, from playing dead, Judy took his front paws in her hands and they danced a waltz together. People clapped and clapped. Last of all, of course, he said his prayers, and after

that he chased his tail again, and then he and Judy ran off the stage together. But everyone clapped so much that they had to come back three times to take bows. Irma clapped louder than all the rest. Judy and Orbit had made her forget her troubles and think only of what a good time she was having.

When Judy came out for the last encore, she stepped to the front of the stage and said, "Please don't forget to vote for Miss Oglethorp's room to get the picture of *Washington Crossing the Delaware*. And be sure to see Irma Baumlein's exhibit of dolls. It's the best thing in the show!"

There was more clapping after that, but Judy and Orbit did not come back again. Next there was a piano solo by a third-grader who played "The March of the Goblins," but in the middle of it he forgot and had to start all over again. "Yes, Judy and Orbit were the best," Irma said to herself. She thought that she would go and find them and tell them how good they had been.

The crowd was thinning again and she was able to push her way over to the place where the steps led up to the stage. By the time she got there, however, Judy had gone and she could not see her. In order to get a better view, Irma climbed up two steps and stood looking out over the audience.

There was some kind of commotion going on at the back of the auditorium. Irma could not see what it was, so she climbed up one step higher. It appeared to be some kind of chase or fight between men, but so many of the audience were running to see too that Irma could not make out what was happening.

"The March of the Goblins" was still going on, plink-plank-plink-plank, on the stage above, but over that sound there now came a sound of shouting.

"Catch him! Catch him! Stop, thief, *stop!*" someone was shouting. Others cried, "Help! Police! Something has been stolen! What's been stolen? What is it?"

Among the many confused cries, Irma heard a voice say, "The Biggest Doll in the World! Irma Baumlein's doll has been stolen!"

Irma felt as if she had been turned to stone. She could not move down a step or up a step. There she stood, frozen stiff, like the marble bust of Great-grandfather Jacob Baumlein, the Man of Integrity.

Then she could see a running figure coming around the auditorium, heading for a side door, and it was *Bob Hickey!* And in his arms he held the *dummy!*

In her body of stone, Irma's heart began to thaw and beat again, very fast. Bob Hickey had found the dummy and he was running away with it! And right behind him came Judy's father, Officer Miller, shouting, "Stop, thief, in the name of the law!"

Women and little girls were screaming. Boys and men were shouting with pleasure as if a TV Western had suddenly come to life. Everywhere there was excitement.

Just before Bob Hickey reached the door, Officer Miller caught him by the collar and prevented him from escaping. The dummy went clattering to the floor, and Irma could see its arm fly off like a curved pink boomerang. Officer Miller had his arm around Bob Hickey's neck in a strangle hold while a helpful bystander snapped the handcuffs around Bob's wrists.

The third-grader had just started "The March of the Goblins" for the third time when Mr. Hardy, the principal, came to the front of the stage and shouted, "Quiet, everybody, quiet! What is going on here?"

People tried to tell him: "Someone was stealing the Biggest Doll in the World. Officer Miller caught him in the act. Look at him! There is the thief!"

Leading poor Bob, whose face was beet red, his hands securely fastened together, Officer Miller elbowed his way through the crowd to the foot of the stage.

"Mr. Hardy," he said, "this man tried to steal one of the most valuable exhibits of the whole show. He was stealing the Biggest Doll in the World. Fortunately he did not get away with it."

"Young man," said Mr. Hardy to Bob Hickey, "what do you have to say for yourself?"

"It's not a doll at all," Bob stammered. "It's a dummy that was stolen from Baumlein's Store. I was just trying to take it back where it belongs."

"My dear chap," said Mr. Hardy, "that is the lamest excuse I have ever heard. Someone call the patrol car, please, so that Officer Miller can haul this fellow off to jail, and we can go on with our program." (The third-grader was starting "The March of the Goblins" for the fourth time, and it did look bad for the completion of the program.)

"Believe me," cried Bob Hickey earnestly, "I'm not a thief. I was just trying to return stolen property to the store where I work."

"A fine tale, that is!" said Officer Miller. "We all know that this is the Biggest Doll in the World and that it belongs to a little girl in Miss Oglethorp's room. How dare you say it isn't?"

"But it isn't!" cried Bob Hickey miserably.

"Take him away," said Mr. Hardy, "and let him tell his story to the judge. A night in jail will give him time to think about the shocking thing he has done."

They were taking Bob Hickey away, and the pretty young lady who had hung on Bob's arm a little earlier in the evening was weeping.

Suddenly Irma found herself running up the final steps to the stage. She ran out beside Principal Hardy and held up her arms.

"Stop!" she cried in the loud voice she used for Aunt Julia. "Stop, everybody! Listen! Don't take him away! Don't!"

Everybody stopped and looked at Irma, even Officer Miller and Bob Hickey and the weeping young lady.

"It's all my fault," Irma shouted. "I never did have

the Biggest Doll in the World. I just said all that. It was
a terrible lie. And I went to Baumlein's Store and I stole
a dummy, and I was going to return it tomorrow. But
don't blame Bob Hickey. He was just trying to take care
of Baumlein property, the way Uncle Arnold told him
to. Please let him go, and you can put the handcuffs on
me instead."

Irma's glasses were all fogged up, but she couldn't
stop to polish them. The many faces below her were
blurred into a misty sea, but she could feel that they
were all looking at her. The crowd gave a long, shudder-
ing sigh, the sound of many people saying, "Ah-h-h-h-h!"

Blindly Irma made her way back to the side of the stage where the stairs went down. She heard Mr. Hardy say, "Officer Miller, in the light of this confession, I believe that you had better release the prisoner."

A great sense of lightness and buoyancy began to fill Irma's body. It was a curious sensation, as if she were a balloon tugging at its string so that it could sail into the stratosphere. The terrible weight that had been holding her down for weeks was gone. She was still a little sad, but she was free.

People began to crowd around her at the foot of the stairs, and at any moment she expected to hear the click of the handcuffs and feel them on her wrists.

Then someone was calling her name. "Irma! Irma! Irma, darling!" Someone put warm arms around her. Irma looked over the top of her foggy glasses, and there, very close to her, was her mother's face, just as it had always looked. And behind her mother was her father's face and two slow tears were running down his cheeks.

# Irma Resolves to Be More Careful

"But how did you get here?" Irma asked, after she had hugged and kissed her mother a dozen times.

"We planned it as a surprise for you, Irma," her mother said. "Your daddy met me at the airplane, but when we got back to the house, you weren't there."

"I see now it was a great mistake," Mr. Baumlein said. "I should have told you that your mother was coming and let you help me look for the little new house where we are going to live. I'm sorry, Irma. Maybe a surprise was not a good idea after all."

"But how did you know where to find me?" Irma asked.

"Mrs. Dillingham helped us," Irma's mother said. "She had found the invitation to the Harvest Home when she emptied your wastebasket. She thought you might be there. And, Irma, she gave me the crumpled letter you had written. Oh, Irma, you must have missed me as much as I missed you!"

"I did," Irma said. "I really did."

Just then Miss Oglethorp came up to shake Irma's hand, and Irma was able to say, "Miss Oglethorp, I'd like to have you meet my parents. They were a little late, but they are here."

"Irma is a very good student," Miss Oglethorp said. "She reads a lot and she knows many difficult words that the other children don't know. We all love Irma very much."

"Even without the doll?" Irma asked timidly. "Even after all I did?"

"What you did tonight was brave enough to erase all of the other mistakes," said Miss Oglethorp seriously.

So Irma took her parents all around and showed them everything—Peter's drawings and Gwen's buttons and Mary's cat. Judy and Orbit and Luke came up and were introduced. Judy said, "I'm glad Troubella has gone back to the store. I never really liked her. And look what has happened to Beep, Irma."

Judy put her arm around Irma, and they went to look at Beep. There she sat in her little chair, all alone behind the screen, and on her breast the judges had pinned a large blue ribbon with a rosette.

"What for?" asked Irma happily.

"For the most interesting antique in the show," said Judy. "Isn't that something?"

Well, of course, with Judy and Orbit, and Rodney's card tricks, and the drawings and rocks and buttons and stamps, and with a blue ribbon pinned on the breast of

BEEP, Miss Oglethorp's class won the right to have *Washington Crossing the Delaware* hanging in their room for the whole coming year. The children were all happy, and no one seemed to mind that the Biggest Doll in the World had gone back to Baumlein's Store where she belonged.

Irma slept late the next morning. She slept so long that her mother came in to awaken her.

"Wake up, darling," Mrs. Baumlein said. "In about an hour Daddy is coming to take us around and show us the new house where we are going to live."

Irma stretched her arms and yawned. She felt very happy this morning. But something was still puzzling her.

"But, Mama," she said, "you look just the same. I'm so glad."

"Why shouldn't I, pet?" asked Mrs. Baumlein, sitting down on the side of Irma's bed.

"Because of having your face lifted."

"Face lifted?" cried Mrs. Baumlein in horror.

"But I heard you say it. You said you would go to a health spa and maybe you would have your face lifted."

Mrs. Baumlein began to laugh.

"Oh, Irma! Irma! You are just like your father—so literal, so sane. But I love you both. I really can't do without you. I found that out all those long weeks when I was alone finishing up that horrid mural."

Irma thought about this in a sane and literal way, and

she came to the conclusion that she must be more like her mother than her mother knew. The Biggest Doll in the World! It was like the Lifted Face, a wild idea that popped full-blown from a creative mind. Only with her mother the wild idea disappeared in a moment like a bubble, while, with Irma, her sane and literal self had tried to carry it through and make a fact of it.

"And, Irma darling," Mrs. Baumlein said, "your father and I have been talking it over, and we have decided to get you for Christmas a real doll as big as you are. We may have to order it made especially, but we want you to have your heart's desire."

"Oh, no!" cried Irma. Suddenly she burst into tears

so that she had to take off her glasses and polish them.

"Why, darling," said her mother, "we thought that was what you wanted."

"Oh, please," said Irma, "all I want is a hamster or a little dog that I can teach tricks to. Please, Mama, don't get me the doll!"

"Darling, you may have the whole backyard of the new house filled from wall to wall with hamsters, and you may have twenty little dogs to teach tricks to. Oh, Irma, I want you to be happy!"

Irma smiled and gave her mother a hug. She knew now that her mother meant that she could have two or three hamsters and one little dog. It was all a manner of speaking.

Still Irma said to herself, "It's dangerous, though. I love my mother just as she is, and for her the things she says aren't lies. But, for myself, I'm going to be more careful in the future."